FACES

FACES

Leigh Kennedy

THE ATLANTIC MONTHLY PRESS
NEW YORK
♦

"The Silent Cradle" was first published in *Shadows* 6 1983;
"Tuning" in *Nantucket Review* 1985;
"The Window Jesus" in *Shayol* 1985;
"Belling Martha," "Greek" and "Her Furry Face" in *Asimov's* 1983.

First published in Great Britain in 1986 by
Jonathan Cape Ltd., London.
First American edition, August 1987.

Library of Congress Cataloging-in-Publication Data

Kennedy, Leigh, 1951–
    Faces.

    I. Title
PS3561.E4266F3   1987   813'.54   86-28812
ISBN 0-87113-140-4

Printed and bound in the United States of America

FIRST PRINTING

DEDICATION

To all my parents –
Betty and Ray Larkin
John Two McClure and the
memory of Jean McClure

/ Contents /

/ The Silent Cradle /

Florie O'Bannon first suspected that she had a third child about mid-October.

The room at the end of the hall had been relegated to storage, mostly furnishings that Vanessa and Tim had grown out of. Florie opened the door, expecting disarray. The old crib that both children had used stood against one wall, a yellow blanket draped across the rail, as if to keep the bright sunlight off the mattress.

There was the smell of soured milk.

Florie stood for a moment, rubbing her arms. Everything had been packed away into the closet except those things an infant would need. A clean, dry bottle stood on the bedside stand, which was filled with folded diapers.

She walked to the window, trying to remember when she'd last come into this room. A month . . . two months ago? She remembered closing the door one evening in late summer to hide the clutter. She opened the window to air out the strange smell.

'Now, why did I come in here?' she asked aloud. She'd completely forgotten. Coming through the window, the breeze was cool. Too cool. Instinctively, she shut the window.

She walked back into the living room, filled with nostalgia about newborns. Vanessa was now eight; Tim five. Both had been a joy to her at all ages, and yet sometimes she thought the newborn's day most magical, like the first days of a love affair. She had only wanted to stare at their wrinkled faces and fondle their toes.

She sat down cross-legged in front of the bookcases where they kept the baby albums.

There was a new one. Like the others, it had a padded white binding. Tentatively, Florie pulled it out and opened it.

Born: October 11, 7:45 a.m., 8 lb., 4 oz., 21½ inches, George Russell O'Bannon.

No picture.

Florie reread the entry absently, trying to imagine what sort of joke her husband might be playing on her. He'd often told her that she enjoyed children too much, that two would certainly be enough. No, this was not the kind of thing he would do. The smell of milk, the casualness of the blanket on the crib . . . These things were apart from his senses, too subtle for his kind of joke.

Florie closed the book and put it away. Momentarily, she felt guilty. Yes, she would love to have another child, and, for a moment, she could pretend. When Tim came storming in from the back yard calling, 'Mom! Mom!' she thought that she might shush him. The baby was sleeping.

But she said nothing. She would wait to see who would finally break down and laugh with her about the book and the room.

Florie paused in the hallway. Vanessa stood at the crib with her face wedged between the side rails. An empty bottle lay in the crib.

'What are you doing?' Florie asked.

Vanessa looked up, embarrassed. 'Just looking,' she said.

'At what?' Florie realized that she sounded sterner than necessary.

Children have a way of looking obviously secretive without knowing the adult ability to follow such nuances. Florie smiled at her daughter's coyness, feeling a flush of recognition for her as an individual. 'Did you put the bottle in there?' Florie saw a thin white residue on one side.

'No.' Vanessa pulled away from the crib and started past Florie without looking up.

'What are you thinking about, little one?' Florie asked.

'Ms Harley asked me how my new little brother was,' she said in a tone of confession.

Florie knelt and looked Vanessa in the eye. 'We don't have a baby,' she said. 'Did you come in here to look?'

Vanessa nodded. 'I thought maybe he was a secret.'

Florie laughed. 'It would be hard to keep that a secret, wouldn't it? Besides, wouldn't I want you to help me with a new baby?'

Vanessa smiled briefly, then a question appeared in her eyes again. 'But what was that sound I heard the other night?'

'What sound?' Florie was chilled.

'It sounded like a baby crying.'

Florie paused to pull herself together. 'It may have been some cats in the yard.'

Vanessa gave her a doubtful look but said nothing. After Vanessa went to the kitchen, Florie looked back at the silent crib. She pulled the door to.

Quietly.

The meatloaf is too salty, she thought, shaking the ketchup bottle over her plate.

'I can't imagine how this got started, Florie,' her husband said. 'Don't they remember the picnic this summer? You were in shorts and a halter top. Don't they remember Bridget's birthday party? That was only a few months ago.'

'Don't know, Bert,' she said.

The children looked from their plates to their parents, forks in their mouths, eyes curious. Tim had a milk moustache.

Florie had hoped her husband would clear up the whole affair. But in the last few minutes, he had proved to be as puzzled as herself. 'Well, whoever it is is close to us,' she said. And she rose to fetch the baby book she'd found.

She discovered new entries: a month-old weight and a note of the six-weeks check-up. 'Healthy!' it said. She found an envelope stuck between the pages. Her husband took the book and leafed through it, frowning. 'What is this?'

She laughed. And then she began to giggle, self-consciously, knowing her amusement wasn't shared yet. Tears wet her lashes.

'Florie?' Bert said. 'What's going on? Are you trying to tell me something?'

She handed him the paper and envelope which she'd just read. 'He's a cheap kid, anyway.'

Bert smiled vaguely as he read the receipt from the pediatrician. Paid. They both ignored Vanessa's persistent, 'What? What is it?'

'Florie, it's a funny joke,' Bert said flatly.

'But it's not mine,' she said, smiling.

Tim looked back and forth between his parents with reserve. 'Mom, can I have more potatoes?'

At Christmas, Florie put a teddy bear under the tree and tagged it 'Russell.' Vanessa wanted it, but Florie playfully viewed it as a sacrifice to the prank. Into the crib it went.

By Easter, it was worn. Florie thought that the children played with it surreptitiously.

By summer, there had been other notes and receipts in the baby book. Florie discovered that Russell cut his first tooth earlier than her other children.

By fall, she found pieces of zwieback on the floor. Anything placed at the edge of counters was likely to be found on the floor.

She said little about it to Bert. In the beginning, they had taken it lightly. But now, she took pleasure in the situation. She no longer thought about who was pulling the prank or why. Now that Tim was in school all day, she'd begun to go shopping, visiting with her mother and a few non-working friends.

She would pause at the door, staring inward, uneasy about leaving.

Whenever she stood in the extra room, she felt a kind of

warm spookiness. As if someone were thinking of her strongly and lovingly. She set up her sewing machine in the room. Then a comfortable chair for reading by the window.

More and more often, she found an excuse to spend time by the crib.

'Florie,' Bert called.

She thought he was in their bedroom, but she found him in the spare room. He was holding a small wooden truck. He looked stern, as he did when he had to do or say something he didn't relish.

'What's the matter?' she asked.

'We can't afford for you to be buying things like this for foolishness.'

'What!' She looked at the truck. Like the mobile that hung over the crib, little blue ducks and yellow fish swimming mid-air, like the rattlers and the teething rings, it had just suddenly been there. Where it had come from, she had no idea.

'Listen, Florie,' Bert said patiently. 'I know you would like to have another baby.'

'Wait a minute,' she said. 'I don't have anything to do with this.'

Bert sighed. 'Why can't you just talk to me about things any more? What's happened to you?'

Florie shook her head. 'You've got it all wrong. I haven't done any of this. Well, I bought the teddy,' she said, picking it up out of the crib. She felt a pang, wondering if somehow she really was responsible for whatever was going on. But how? She knew in her mind that soon a friend, her mother, or even Vanessa would own up to it.

'We can't afford this joke any more,' Bert said.

Florie was aware that things were tight. Their car had thrown a rod a few months ago and they'd unexpectedly been forced to buy a new one. They'd had to have the plumber out a few times. School clothes were expensive this year, and Christmas was on the way. Prices were going up.

'Bert, believe me,' Florie said.

He studied her a long while. 'I don't know what to say. I think we need for you to go back to work, even just for half days.'

'Bert . . .'

He put his arms around her, teddy and all. 'I think it would be good for you. I suspect you're bored.'

Stunned, Florie said nothing. Perhaps he was right.

She sat at her desk and squirmed. As if she itched, she longed to scratch, but she couldn't localize it. She simply was uncomfortable.

She pleaded illness and rushed home. In the bathroom, a tub of cloudy tepid water stood, and a box of baking soda sat on the floor. Florie looked in the spare room. It was hot and stuffy, but she didn't dare open the window.

She lay on her bed, feeling safe at home, but worried. Worried about what, she didn't know. She dozed.

As she slept, she seemed to be aware of her sleeping self, knowing where she was and why. And in that awareness, she held close to her the shape of a toddler wrapped in a blanket. The child was restless, his fever radiated through the blanket to her.

'It's all right, Russell,' she said in her sleep. She comforted him just as she had Vanessa and Tim, thanking God that she had already had chicken-pox.

She was furious the day she came home and the kitchen was ravaged. Pots and pans, dishes and tin cans had been pulled out of the cupboards. A stick of butter hadn't yet melted enough to hide the teeth marks.

She yelled at Russell from the living room, to be sure that he heard her from wherever he was. But he was too young to understand yet, for the situation didn't improve until the receipts from the daycare center began arriving.

'Mom,' Tim said, 'Russell broke the crib.'

Florie looked at Bert.

Bert stood. 'Now, look, young man. That's going too far. You can't blame things on an imaginary being. What did you do?'

'I didn't do it,' Tim said with the certainty of a clear conscience. 'I heard a noise a while ago and now the crib's busted. Come and look.'

Florie saw that Bert believed Tim's honesty, but not the story. They followed him into Russell's room. The slats of the crib had been smashed outward.

'The bed's too small for him now,' she said calmly.

'That's stupid,' Bert said. 'I think . . .' He shrugged. 'This whole thing is stupid.' And he stalked away.

They bought Timothy a new bed, had the crib hauled away and sent Tim's old bed into the extra room. Florie went to the second-hand store and bought a bedspread for the old bed. She cleaned out the baby things and had a garage sale. All of Tim's old clothes went into Russell's dresser.

Sometimes she found them in the laundry hamper.

Tim spent time playing in Russell's room. Bert noticed it, explaining that Tim probably missed his old bed. (Bert never did see the need for the new one.) 'Besides,' he said, 'we don't yell at him when he bounces on it any more.'

Vanessa found blood on the back porch one day. A few days later a receipt came for nine stitches at the clinic.

Bert raged. 'I've had enough of this!'

He called Dr Thorn. After explaining the 4-year-old prank to the pediatrician whom Florie had always been reluctant to discuss it with, the doctor only said, 'I don't know what to tell you. According to our records, Russell has always been seen by my partner, who only works on Wednesday afternoons.'

'What the *hell* is going on around here?'

'I don't know, Mr O'Bannon. Maybe you should hold a seance.'

Florie heard Bert say something she thought improper

and impolite. Embarrassed, she took her children to another pediatrician the next time.

One day the kitchen window was shattered by a baseball. Vanessa and Tim were not home. Florie saw no one in the yard.

Everyone disavowed responsibility for the leftovers being set out for a persistent stray dog. Eventually the dog won his way into the family. He never answered to any name they gave him, and always slept on Russell's bed. Much later, he got a silver tag and they found out that his name was Claude. Claude was a quiet dog; he always seemed to be waiting and listening.

Vanessa told Florie matter-of-factly that Russell would sometimes at night come into her room and hold her hand. In fact, Vanessa seemed to be his favorite. She found unexplained treats in her room – sometimes candy, sometimes a new comic book. On her sixteenth birthday, she received a record. It was Vanessa who'd started long ago having a birthday celebration every October for her youngest brother.

When Russell started school, Tim tried dutifully (on Florie's instruction) to check on Russell in class. Tim was too bashful to speak to the teachers. He peeked in the windows, but saw no one he could positively identify as his brother. So Florie tried herself. He was always either on a field trip, or out of the room working on a special project.

Florie found report cards in his room, along with the baseballs, comic books, jars of grasshoppers, magnifying glasses, bits of junk picked up along the walk from school to home. He was a good student, though, 'shy and hard to communicate with verbally,' as his second-grade teacher put it.

He left his parents cards on the dinner table every holiday.

Russell was treated like a fact by the children. What to them had been a bit of amusement that their parents had thought up turned into a person who had never quite arrived or had just left. Russell's doings were reported at the dinner table.

Florie had forgotten that it was a joke. When people asked her about her children, she would say, 'I have three . . .' and hesitate, or she would say she had two and be just as uncertain.

Bert didn't see it their way. The evening before Russell's eighth birthday, Bert stopped Vanessa mid-sentence as she talked about the cake she was going to bake.

'Enough!' he shouted.

Florie, Vanessa and Tim stared, each shaken.

'There is no Russell, there never has been a Russell, and there never will be,' Bert said, leaning towards Vanessa. 'You,' he said to Florie, 'have two children. *Two*, Florie. This one,' – he pointed to Vanessa, then to Tim – 'and this one. I have no son named Russell.'

'Aw, Dad,' Tim said, as if this were an old argument.

'Show me,' Bert said, pounding his fist on the table. 'Show me!'

'Vanessa, why don't you and Tim clean up the kitchen,' Florie said. She stood and held out her hand to Bert. 'Let's take a walk.'

Bert sat at the table until Florie brought him his jacket. He put it on and walked out of the house ahead of her. They strolled silently for a time. Florie took his hand.

Bert kicked at some leaves. 'You take it for granted. I just can't. Eight years, Florie. I just can't stand it any more. It's not funny, and yet I can't take it seriously. You can't really believe all this, can you?'

Florie shrugged. 'You remember what I told you about my family? When we were growing up, the door would blow open and someone would say, "It's our ghost." And we said our ghost took things, broke things, did this or that. It just became something we said. I don't know, love. Maybe it's the same one, only now he's got a name and a place.'

Bert looked at her. 'Well, is he real or not?'

Florie paused.

'Is he real?' Bert insisted.

'I . . . don't know.'

He shrugged.

After a silence, he said, 'You know, I've been thinking about something old Dr Thorn said years ago. Something we should have done sooner.'

'What's that?'

Bert laughed a little. He hesitated long enough to let Florie know that he was embarrassed. 'Maybe we should have a seance.'

They both laughed. Florie took his arm, and felt good that they were laughing together. 'Are you serious? she asked, still giggling.

'Oh, I don't know, love. It couldn't hurt.'

They heard a rustle of dried leaves in the yard as they passed. Both looked, but neither saw anything. Bert frowned as he swung Florie back toward the house.

Then they laughed as they ran.

If there could be a medium with respectability, references, and an honest, no hocus-pocus air, it was Barbara. She was young, slim, blonde, and straightforward. Florie had found her through a psychiatrist's reference and checked her out thoroughly.

First, she listened with a pen and notepad to the whole story. She looked at Russell's room, handled some of his possessions, scrutinized his handwriting carefully. Florie felt odd watching those long fingers touching his things, as if that made Russell more real. Quietly, Barbara asked what kind of person they thought he was, and everyone agreed that he was a good kind of kid – no one ever complained. He'd only done things that any boy would do. Florie chuckled about the worms in the kitchen sink (in retrospect).

Barbara sat and explained to all of them that seances

didn't often work. Rarely, in fact. But there seemed to be a strong possibility of a ghost. Why, she didn't know, unless there was some strong desire for this addition to the family that had attracted Russell.

Florie looked at her hands, guiltily avoiding Bert's face. She shivered. She realized that she'd never thought of Russell as a *ghost*, really. More a *spirit*.

'Well, do you think this is a good idea?' Barbara asked. 'Suppose we do contact him?'

Florie and Bert looked at one another. Florie tried to figure out her feelings about it; Bert seemed to be watching her face for the answer.

'Shall we go ahead?' Barbara asked patiently.

Florie gave Bert an 'I-don't-see-why-not' look and he nodded.

'I don't see why not' he said.

Barbara joked with Tim about his cold hands as they sat down at the dining room table. Tim's bashfulness was apparent even in the dim light. Barbara talked calmly to Russell, asking him to appear. She spoke to him as if he were shy. Then she turned to Vanessa. 'You talk to him.'

Vanessa stared at the table. 'It won't work.'

Barbara raised her eyebrows just a little. 'Why not?'

'Because . . .' She looked at Barbara in that quiet way that adolescent girls look at young women. 'Seances are for *dead* people.'

The hairs on the back of Florie's neck rose.

The family looked at Barbara for the answer. Barbara half-smiled as she considered. 'Maybe you're right.'

Florie glanced at Bert, who sighed. He looked worn, and just a bit depressed. Barbara let go of Tim and Vanessa's hands. 'Why don't we rest up. And if you decide you want to try again, we'll get together another night.' She stood.

They were quiet as they watched her gather her notes almost absently. 'Keep in touch,' she said as she left.

Florie woke and reached out into the space beside her in the bed. She listened for a while to the early morning sounds, trying to discover the movement of her husband in the house somewhere. She slid out of the warm covers and padded through the room into the hallway. Softly, she called Bert's name.

The door to Russell's room was slightly open. Quietly, she pushed it wide. Bert sat in a chair by the bed. He lifted his sleepy chin from his chest and looked at her bleary-eyed. He put his finger to his lips.

They returned to their room. 'What is it?' she whispered, climbing back into bed.

'I'm not sure. I think he had a nightmare or something.'

He held her as they fell asleep again. Florie felt something had changed, but Bert never talked much about it again.

When Vanessa went to college, Russell missed her so much that he apparently spent his evenings in her room reading; his books were sometimes in a neat stack by her bed. Claude took to napping on her rug, too.

Tim became interested in computers in high school and found that his brother borrowed his magazines and books on the subject. Tim said that he figured sometimes Russell went to Willie's with him. Willie had a micro-computer. They sometimes found funny messages on the screen. When Florie asked what kind off messages, Tim told her that Russell suggested a computer game of hide-and-seek which they worked out and had a lot of fun with.

Florie was more embarrassed when she found the men's magazines under Russell's bed than she ever had been about finding Tim's. (She had been sure she was alone when she found Tim's.)

Tim went off to college.

Russell liked his schoolwork; his reports were always excellent. While a junior in high school he won an essay award, which Florie found on his dresser and framed on his wall. He left his term papers out, which Florie and Bert read with amazement. He seemed fascinated with international relations, history, and economics.

'Oh, Bert,' Florie said once, 'what if he goes into espionage?'

Bert assured her that he might be elusive, but he left too many clues to be a spy.

His high school yearbooks showed up on the bedroom bookshelf. Russell O'Bannon was always listed – in fact, he belonged to the computer club, Latin club, and Honor Society. He was never available for photos, however.

In the summer of his eighteenth year, the house became uncommonly lonely. Claude wagged his tail wistfully every now and then as he sniffed through Russell's room. Florie expanded her part-time job to full-time. It wasn't easy at first to enjoy the new solitude. The holidays were the same as ever; Christmas brought a full round of presents, including gifts from Russell. He'd developed a real knack for getting something for everyone that they'd never really wanted but was a marvelous gift just the same.

Bert and Florie received the paid tuition notices from a prestigious and expensive university. Russell was apparently doing several part-time jobs during the school year, including gopher work at a law firm.

He attended Vanessa's wedding, but didn't make it back for summer vacation of his second year.

It was that summer, his twentieth year, that the mailgram from Italy came.

'Look,' Florie said, waving it at Bert. They had been receiving postcards from England, France and Spain for the last month. Without a close look, she tore the thin envelope open.

Florie went numb. She sat down with the letter fluttering in her hand.

'What is it?' Bert asked.

He took the letter from her.

They wept, then called Vanessa and Tim.

Russell had been killed in a terrorist explosion at a small Italian airport. The American Embassy had written, expressing terrible regret for their loss, and that the students he'd been traveling with had said only wonderful things about their brilliant young son.

Florie found Bert sitting on Russell's bed. She sat down beside him and leaned her cheek against his shoulder.

She decided then that they would keep the room just as it had been when Russell was alive.

/ Max Haunting /

Max was great in 1967.

Some people have an instinctive feel for what's right at the time – how long to grow hair, whether to take up recorder or guitar, or both, how much acid to drop, whether to stay away from speed, when to flip the bird to the pigs or be honey-sweet. Max was always right in every situation. He was great at parties, marches, sit-ins, love-ins, concerts, even haylofts. He could talk Rilke, Sartre, Leary, Thoreau, Tolkien and Heinlein, and yet swear with the vitality of a pirate. He understood comparative political systems and could expertly critique Marx's historical materialism. Everyone loved Max; he was a guru, a Buddha, a preacher. He made his friends laugh. He made the dim night gatherings hush with profound thought, interwoven with cannabis and thick sandalwood smoke. He fascinated the chicks, who gladly sewed American flags upside-down on his weary but persistent jeans.

Ten years later, Max was an old song. Cherished, occasionally hummed, good for those nights when one finds the moon, surprised, while stepping out into the back yard to dump the chicken bones that have funked up the kitchen. An old song floating and elusive, shining like that white moon, and oh, so . . . *so* far away. To see Max again made those pent-up wings itch.

Max started showing up on doorsteps, an embodiment of the forgotten lyric.

'Max!' she says.

Max always accepted whatever other people wanted to do, wear, and eat, so long as they loved him, but it surprised him to see Sandra or Freaky or Go-to-town Goldie standing in the doorway with her blonde/brown/auburn hair cut into a sporty wedge/blown-dry/curling-ironed. Her luscious/chubby/skinny body decorated with a tweed pantsuit/polyester housedress/light blue silk that could have come from her mother's closet (but her mother was too big).

'Peace, lovely lady,' he said to Sandra on the first stop. 'You look beautiful. Far out.' Max grinned and pushed his fingers nervously through the brown beard that lay upon his stud-decorated denim jacket. His long, strong fingers poked out of the beard like pink spikes. He noticed the embrace wasn't as eager as in the Old Days.

'Come in!' she said.

'Hey, sure, love. Whata *place*. *Whata* place.' And he was ushered into the living room. Everyone had *furniture* these days. Sandra went Early American, always being the kind to stick to old-fashioned things. She'd married Watermeter, whose alias in the Seventies was Gary. Gary taught welding in a community college after having abandoned his graduate work in Eastern Studies.

'Lucky you caught me here,' Sandra said. 'This is my day off.'

'Working.' Max nodded sagely. 'Everyone's working. Nobody feeds panhandlers any more. Nobody throws quarters into the hat any more for a good street song.'

Sandra laughed and it reminded Max of the night he'd met her in a coffee house, reciting Dylan Thomas from atop a painter's ladder with a spotlight shining on that golden hair. Her hair had floated like exotic feathers around her square face, across her strong shoulders and down over those well-shaped tits that never needed a bra even if she'd elected to wear one. In those days, you could tell a woman that you admired her tits and she would laugh because you were so honest, but never, never was she offended. At least, Sandra never had been.

'Well, Max, what're you doing these days?'

Max sank deep into the chair with nice padded arms and a bright crewel design. He crossed his leg over his knee and reached into his jacket for his stash and papers. 'Still drifting.' he said, rolling a joint.

'Hey, it's been a long time,' Sandra said, watching him from her place in the middle of the sofa with the matching crewel upholstery. She perched there, her rear on the front half of the cushion, maybe nervous, maybe wanting to be those ten inches closer to an old friend.

Max looked up and realized she was talking about the dope, so he handed her the joint for the first hit. 'What do you do when it's your day on?' he asked.

'What? Oh. I'm a psychiatric social worker,' she croaked, holding the vapors under her larynx.

Max laughed.

She explained that their kid, Ravi Shankar Thomas (who now is called Tom) was in the third grade, but Sandra had gone back to graduate school from the time the Americans pulled out of Vietnam until just last year.

'Hard work,' she said slowly, her shoulders rounding as she looked about her. It seemed as if the living room had suddenly become a strange place to her.

'Hey, remember the time we were selling newspapers on the street and the string broke on the skirt you had that laced up the side?' Max was fond of that memory. That was just before Watermeter came into their world with his God-awful sitar playing and chanting. He hadn't known what the hell he was doing, but it had impressed the feathers off Sandra.

Sandra wriggled uncomfortably. 'God,' she said, 'how mortified I was.'

'It was great. I loved it – lacing you up in public.'

She smiled vaguely. 'You don't know what seeing you does to me, Max. Kinda hurts in a way to see that you still carry that magic around with you. You still have a revolutionary gleam in your eyes, you still look like you're ready to hassle Capitol Hill for your rights. Things are so different now. Can't believe it was me, you know. I guess we all have to raise a little hell when we're young.'

'Raise a little hell! We were a revolution! A cultural movement. You and Watermeter and . . .' He couldn't say that other name yet. He took a hit off the joint before eating the roach, an old habit left over from the days before even cops smoked dope. 'I think we changed the world.'

Sandra looked at him dreamily. 'You know, I just remembered how proud I was the time I found myself in the newspaper photo of a peace rally. Oh, the only way I knew it was me was that I'd worn my best black hat with three ostrich feathers, a black velvet jacket, paisley jeans, and engineer boots. I walked next to the "No War Toys For Children" sign. My mother couldn't have picked me out, but I was so sure that the FBI had that picture blown up with a big red circle around me. We thought our phones were tapped, remember? Damn, we sure were important, weren't we?'

Max caught the irony in her voice. 'Yes. We were.' He remembered Sandra's velvet jacket. And the hat playfully placed on someone else's head.

'Have you seen Jenna lately?' she asked casually.

'Jenna,' he repeated, though he hadn't meant to. 'No, but Sandy, we did change the world. Look at this.' Having earlier rifled through the magazines on the coffee table, he remembered a gem or two. 'Greenpeace. Did your parents worry about whales, huh? Did they read *The Humanist*? Do you use insecticides or chilli powder to keep the tomato worms out of your garden? Do you allow your son to model himself upon the violence and intellectual desolation of television programming?'

Sandra's laughter came back, smelling of smoke and incense, sounding like beaded doorways, feeling like leather and fur, rubbing his temples with memory.

The first time he saw Jenna . . .

He was with several people, including Sandra and Watermeter. They had gotten more than a bit stoned, which led to a severe case of the munchies unrelieved by a sparse supply of sunflower seeds and fig bars. They walked down the avenue, singing Grateful Dead songs with their thirsty throats, impressing themselves. One of the girls – Rosemary – wore brass Indian bells on her boots. Max played his harmonica soulfully, thinking how bluesy an A-harp sounded echoing off the city streets.

'Hey, that's the place where Pete and Hellspirit were hassled last night,' Watermeter said, pointing to a coffee shop set in a white rock garden with plastic juniper bushes.

'Let's go,' Max said.

'Yeah!' Rosemary skipped, child-like. 'I haven't had a real hassle for a while.'

'Our dimes are as good as General Hershey's, huh?' Max said. Then he put his arm around Rosemary and whispered, 'Why didn't you speak up? I could have hassled you earlier.' And the way she smiled back at him, he figured she would sleep with him that night.

A waitress met them at that crucial point equal to the cash register. She wore too much make-up, teased her hair into an uneven ball on top of her head, where a tiny white cap hung by a black bobby pin. Pressing menus close to her breasts like a shield, she wore an orange checkered uniform.

'We don't serve hippies here,' she said firmly.

'Well, that's all right,' Max replied sweetly. 'We don't want hippies anyway, we want some cheeseburgers.'

They had to show their money and the manager approved their service provided they each made a dollar minimum order. They were seated near the kitchen in a semi-circular booth after the waitress inspected their feet for shoes.

'Hey, Max, that was far fucking out, man,' Stash whispered.

They giggled for a while, sobered when the waitress came, then giggled again about the coffee, the cream pitcher, the man at the counter. Everything was beautiful, man, everybody loved everybody. It was a free world, in spite of the pigs, the FBI, the draft, and President Johnson.

And then Max lifted his head and saw her in a booth across from them, smiling when they laughed, but alone and stirring her coffee as if that were something important to be done.

At first, he just watched her, amazed at how much hair could grow on a delicate head like that, incredible amounts of dark brown waves and wavelets. Then a mouth that wanted to smile openly, but didn't dare. Just didn't dare. She wore a black turtleneck, a necklace of minute green, yellow and amber beads, jeans, one big turquoise ring like a baby tortoiseshell encased in silver, and grey desert boots.

'Hey, it's one of our people sitting over there,' Max said, 'I'm going to invite her over.'

'Max . . .' Rosemary said.

Max walked to her table. The girl still stared at her coffee as if she either didn't see him or had expected him and waited for a signal. 'Want to join us?' he asked.

She looked up at him and he saw that she was young and fearful and pleased all in one. She shrugged slightly and smiled.

He sat down beside her in the booth. She moved a little but still he felt her maneuvering nervously so as not to touch his ribs. That was not the first time he smelled patchouli, but it was the first time he smelled Jenna's patchouli. 'My name's Max.'

'Hi,' she said.

'Well?' He grinned at her.

'Uh . . . Jenna.' A quick smile then a glance around the coffee shop.

'Waiting for someone?'

'No. Well . . .'

He had to lean closer to hear her. 'What?'

'Unless I was waiting for you and didn't know it.'

'Far out,' he said, studying her. That was a good answer. This little lady had some super vibes. 'Come and sit with us.'

'Okay.' She carried her coffee cup to their table. Max made a round of introductions. For a while the others talked and Jenna said nothing. When Max looked at her, she would smile quickly, but she never said anything. Rosemary grabbed his thigh under the table, but it seemed a last desperate effort. Everyone sensed what was in Max's eyes.

He bought her a cheeseburger which she wolfed down in the most mannerly way a long-hungry person could handle.

As they walked out of the coffee shop, he asked, 'Do you have a place to stay?' Fully aware of the disgusted scowls the group gathered from other customers on their way out, Max waved goodbye to several of them, who looked the other way.

'Not exactly,' she said.

'You can crash with me.' They lagged behind the others, swimming out into the warm night. 'Well, if you don't want to crash *with* me, I can sleep on the floor or something. Door's open anyway.'

She didn't answer then.

They returned to Sandra and Watermeter's place in the same old house with Max's room. Rosemary read Stash's tarot; Watermeter started droning with his sitar (where did he get the money for that thing anyway?); Sandra lay back in sleepy thoughtfulness after they'd passed a pipe. Phil Ochs succeeded Joan Baez with a soft clap of disc upon disc. Jenna leaned against the wall. A blue-faced portrait of Krishna hung above her. Two candles illuminated the smoky room just enough to keep someone from kissing the wrong lips.

Max touched her hand and her slender fingers responded, easing into his grasp comfortably. He grinned at her; she gave a little smile at her toes.

Sandra sat back on the big sofa, looking a bit brighter between the golden wings of her hairdo. 'Well, really, Max, times have changed, haven't they?'

'What?' He felt he'd missed something, but when he tried to think about it, he figured it was just the grass.

'Tell me what you're doing these days,' she said.

'Flowing with the motion of life,' he answered, grinning, pulling his fingers through his beard again. 'Hey, look, Sandy, I can see that you're wiped out. Mind if I fix myself some tea?'

Sandra didn't have any tea except an old store-brand orange pekoe which had been left loose in the cupboard so long that the tea tasted like ginger snaps. Her cupboards held sugar, cake mixes, hamburger instant meals, canned soups, coffee that was more like cocoa than coffee. He noticed when he returned and she was coming back from the bathroom that her ass seemed bigger than it used to be and her hair was dry and stiff. A picture of the kid who used to be Ravi looked like any fourth-grader in the nation. In the family portrait on the television, Watermeter looked like a Gary after all.

'Hey, I gotta go, Sandy. Sorry I missed the family. Maybe next time.'

She allowed him a kiss on the cheek, but his beard seemed to tickle her. He saw her rub her face as he stepped backward, waving reluctantly at the Sandra who stood in those Montgomery Ward shoes.

Freaky was still Freaky only more so in a domesticated way. Her kitchen was a pit – smelled like the armpit of someone who ate onions three, four times a day. The kitchen table was covered with plants and little baby food jars with cuttings of Coleus, Elephant's Ears, and Swedish Ivy. She did the dishes while Max sat in the metal-frame vinyl chair and smoked two joints. Two little kids that seemed somehow the same size and morality but were not twins destroyed the living room while Freaky talked.

'Max, it's so far out to see you. Far out, jeez, I haven't said that for a long time. Hey, don't you miss old times? Do you think about them a lot? Max, you look just the same, I can't believe it. You gotta stay and meet my old man. It's really weird, he was going through the same trip we went through at the same time only a thousand miles away. You know? Sometimes I think we had some sort of telepathic link, but nothing that worked on our conscious minds. We've compared dates and found out that there were times when we were doing the same thing at the same moment. Weird, huh?'

'All you did was eat and screw and smoke, Freaky,' Max said affectionately, recalling some of the solidly sexy times in the garage of her apartment house (the landlady didn't allow male visitors). Usually during midterm and finals week. Freaky became very active at those times. Every gentle head who lived within a hundred miles found studying difficult with Freaky's aura glowing.

'Wow, Max, seeing you brings it back. You were good. *Good*. I used to love you a lot, you know? I mean, like I wanted you to want just me and all that possessive crap. That was before Jenna . . .'

Jenna.

'. . . but things turned out okay for me. How are you doing, Max? Have you seen Jenna? She's still down there, I heard. Had some problems, but you should go see her, too. Cheer her up.' Freaky wiped the refrigerator vigorously with a soapy sponge, possibly just realizing that the house was a mess. 'Man, you were the best. I can remember some really fine all-nighters with you.'

Max felt that he had to stop her. 'I wish you wouldn't talk about me like that. Sounds like I'm dead or something.'

Then he realized his mistake when Freaky's eyes lit up. 'Oh, no, Max. I didn't mean that at all. Hey, you know?'

'You know what I mean,' he said softly. She looked away because she wasn't sure. Max realized that he was confused, too.

Jenna had been so easy to talk to, so easy to live with.

The two of them had sunned in the park, denimed thighs

touching, lying on their stomachs; he was reading his sociology texts, she was reading *The Art of Loving* by Erich Fromm. Down the hill an informal group hootenannied. Jenna stopped reading and nestled her chin among the knuckles of her intertwined hands.

'You know what I really like about you?' he'd said suddenly.

'Hmm?' She smiled, but didn't immediately look up from her book.

'You enjoy everything. There isn't anything that I drag you along to do with me that you don't seem to like. Even when I do homework.'

She turned her head so that her cheek lay on her hands and squinted up at him. 'I like what you do.'

He took the grass blade out of his mouth to kiss her, then they listened to the singing. Songs of the weary coal miners, of yearning maidens, of freedom, of the Irish rising to fight under the moon.

'I'm grateful,' she said. 'You know how parents always tell you to say "thank you" and "please" and smile to be polite. Well, I'd like to say thank you, Max, but that doesn't sound like the way I feel. You make my life beautiful.'

He thought about the night he'd explained existential philosophy to her, defending his own agnosticism, laying bare the meaninglessness of the cosmos, ripping to shreds any ounce of soul or spirit that existed outside one's own making. At first she listened with startled eyes, then later he found her in the dark – tears on her face.

'Max, Max, we're so little!' she whispered, 'so unimportant, so *little*.'

And still, she was grateful to him.

'Jenna, my little bird,' Max said, concentrating fully on her when at any other time he would have half his mind on the harmonica. The park dissolved. 'I love you,' he said, after days of wanting to.

She didn't answer. That's the way it was when something

meant a lot to her. She listened to the words intensively and thought carefully about what it all signified. Later, he knew, he would hear her answer, but it was enough that she leaned against his shoulder, as if to assure him that she was aware.

Freaky had lots of peppermint tea and made some stone-ground carob cookies and whole wheat noodles and boiled eggs in apple curry. Her old man, Carver – which was his last name but that was what Freaky called him – came home and they snorted and lay on the living room floor and talked about the street light coming through the picture window smeared with silvery baby hand-prints. And Freaky held Max's hand. She asked Carver shyly if he thought it would be funny if she and Max had a roll in the hay for old times' sake and Carver said, yeah, it would be funny all right. But something in his voice made Freaky hesitate, so Max fell asleep and woke up the next morning when one of the kids stuck a toy wheel dripping with cookie-saliva in his ear. Carver said something about calling into work sick, but Max understood. They smoked one more joint and he left.

Freaky's eyes were tearful when he turned away from her.

Goldie kept the house after the divorce from What's-his-name. She liked antiques; mixed with glass, chrome, leather furniture were Japanese platters, a grandfather clock, fragile chairs, tapestry. 'I redid this,' Goldie said, stroking an old desk. Her hands moved like they were onstage or posing for black-and-white photography. Max thought Go-to-town Goldie had gotten even thinner, a compulsion not to be like her mother. Her hip bones showed. Her nipples showed, but that was lucky because she'd nearly dieted her bosom out of existence.

'Nice.'

'Do you still do some carpentry, Max?' she asked, her hazel eyes looking at him sideways over the angle of her cheek. Auburn hair moved like a shimmering forest around her head. Like the antique chairs, she also seemed fragile. Max had never felt completely at ease with Goldie, though he was the one to tag her 'Go-to-town' because of the way she dressed. Sweeping, graceful, like a dancer. He'd introduced her to the Underground crowd early, finding her in a philosophy class. She went deeper underground than any of his close friends, and they had stopped talking politics in 1966.

'Some,' he said.

'How is Jenna?'

'I don't know.'

'Oh, too bad.'

Jenna hadn't met Goldie until she and Max had been together for several months.

Goldie always had furniture, even when the rest of the college population sat on cushions, slept on mattresses, had brick and board bookcases. Goldie had a brass bed, a maple rocker, an old desk, and an honest pine bookcase.

He remembered Jenna sitting on the edge of the brass bed, shyly complimenting Goldie on the patchwork quilt. Sunny, the bedroom yielded nothing about Goldie's personal habits other than orderliness. Her clothes hung in the closet. No mirrors, no birth control devices, no wine glasses, no pipe, no photos of Mama or Cousin Annie. Just the bed and Jenna bouncing lightly with her feet bare on the wooden floor.

'Would you like some wine?' Goldie had asked, turning out of the room.

'No, thank you,' Jenna said.

Max stood by the bed and contemplated Jenna. She was pale, introspective, listless lately. He worried. He suspected. 'I'll have some,' he said.

'Of course, Max, you never turn anything down.'

Max and Jenna smiled at one another, left alone. Then

Jenna lay back, her feet still touching the floor. Finally, he asked, 'What's the matter?'

'I don't think Goldie likes me.'

'Aaa, Goldie,' he said disparagingly. 'She likes everyone equally but from a distance. Nothing personal.' He sat on the bed, half his butt on the pillows so that he balanced by putting one hand on Jenna's shoulder.

'What does it mean to say "crossing the Rubicon?" ' she asked, staring up at the ceiling.

'It means doing something that tells the rest of the world to go to hell because you're going to do what you planned anyway, whether they like it or not. Why?'

'Where did it come from?' She reached across to his arm, guiding it so that he leaned over her, his hand on the far side of her.

'Julius Caesar.'

'How do you know all these things?'

Max shrugged. 'Heard about it, read it . . . I don't know.'

She made a face. 'I'm so stupid.'

Max sighed. He didn't know what to say when over and over again she berated herself. True, she had astonishing gaps in her knowledge (another example of the failure of the public school system to educate an intelligent girl), but she read continuously and asked him question after question. Sometimes he had to save them and refer to a friend, or the library.

'Jenna,' he said impatiently.

'Please don't!' She cupped her hands over her face. 'I don't know how you stand me. I'm sorry. I'll shut up.'

'No, listen to me.'

She pulled herself up into a sitting position, using his arm as a stable pillar. For a moment she stared. Then she began to pale to a chalky hue so that her eyes filled up her face with their contrasting darkness. 'Oh, I feel awful,' she said, as if her tongue didn't quite work.

Then she passed out completely.

Goldie had been waiting for a date when Max arrived. Dressed like an Edwardian wedding parcel, smelling like a mysterious flower that probably only grew in the shade of certain rare trees, blooming every three years. She still put him at a loss for words. Why had he come? Because she had been *there*. She had been exquisite, posing as in her ballet exercises at the edge of the fountain dressed only in grace. Go-to-town Goldie arrested for indecent exposure, but treated like a Martian princess even by the pigs. Max had sung himself hoarse in the street collecting money to pay her fine.

He'd never touched her. He didn't know if anyone had.

He wondered if the long gone What's-his-name had either. It would be grounds for a divorce after only three months, wouldn't it?

'Max, look at you.'

'How can I, Goldie? When I look in the mirror, I see only a reflection of myself, not the reality of Max. But then, what is perceived is the flesh, the mere passing illusion of Max. What is Max? Where may I find this elusive vision of self, the *maya* . . .'

'Stop it.'

He did, smiling, sipping the brandy that he'd settled on because he liked to drink from those huge snifters.

Goldie looked at her watch. Where did they make straps that small? He wondered if she had to punch holes in the black leather to fit that skeletal wrist. He envisioned Goldie in the kitchen, a nut-pick in hand, stabbing her watchband with her tongue stuck out in concentration. No . . .

'You're brilliant and talented, just wasting your life away. What have you done?'

'I changed the world in my day,' he said, toasting her with his brandy. 'The world still changes because of things we did and said, don't you think?'

'We didn't change it enough, then. It's all gone sour. You're a vagrant, for God's sake, Max, living off memories of your youth. It's over.'

'All right. I'll go down to the Pentagon next week and apply for a generalship.'

Goldie smirked, a semi-circular crease appearing like a parenthesis at the corner of her mouth. 'You've always been very contrary, Max.'

'I disagree.' He put the brandy down and sank his hands into his jeans pockets. They both looked at the floor, then Max laughed. He held his hand out to her. 'Bye, Go-to-town Goldie.'

'Max, you could've been – '

' – an accountant.' He bowed, kissing her hand. 'I thank you for allowing me to haunt you.'

'Haunt me!' she said, half-laughing, half-uneasy.

But he saw that something in her eyes. The shadows had moved in the mirror, the highway post had taken on a pleading pair of arms, the faucet gushed on its own. Max was a ghost and it amused him.

After he left Goldie, he found the old hill overlooking the city. He took his guitar off the front seat of the Volkswagen bug and sat on the papery grass, singing Dylan, Andersen, Hardin, Lightfoot, Odetta, and Traditional to the smog-flickering lights of the urban civilization below.

He remembered things again.

Jenna and her magically wild, coffee brown hair. She was not pretty, but she was not un-pretty, either. Furtive brown eyes, a nervously laughing mouth. A passionate mouth. She had been a runaway, something Max hadn't been aware of for a long time. But the only difference between Jenna and a lot of people was that she was a child running away. The rest were adults running away.

Parents still got upset when college kids – crazed hippie freaks – made tender love to their willing daughters.

'Hell.' He slammed his hand on the guitar strings, smelling diesel in the wind that had once been fragrant with patchouli and sandalwood from Jenna's throat and wrists and clothes. 'I didn't know she was only fifteen,' he said aloud, defending himself again. Perhaps her parents were dead in their graves now. Perhaps Jenna was married again, busy, uninterested, changed. It didn't matter. For ten years, Max had defended himself.

But now it seemed incredible to Max that Jenna was twenty-five *now* and had been fifteen *then*. She was twenty-five when he knew her; she would be twenty-five when she was eighty. Jenna was Jenna, an unchanging concept.

'No,' he said. He thought of Sandra/Freaky/Goldie. They had changed, hadn't they? Sandra. Freaky. Goldie. No. Well . . . some. Not much. A little. A lot.

How many times had he found Jenna's phone number in these past years? He was each time stricken with a kind of palsy when he started to dial. His hand shook so hard he could not hold the receiver. He'd gotten angry at that hand. Damn you, hold this phone for me. It fluttered, it became boneless and filled with tepid water. He had even paid a kid on the street to call her parents from a phone booth. The kid did it, but Max felt his derision – who is this old fart who can't even call his girlfriend? Her parents hadn't known her address then, either.

'She said Jenna doesn't stay in touch,' the kid told him. 'Last she heard, she moved downtown after her husband split.'

'Husband,' Max said. That was the first he'd heard of Jenna's marriage.

He strummed for a while, his butt getting tired of the hard ground. Thinking of the one-room apartment that he and Jenna had lived in for only four months. Fried potatoes, lentil soup, molasses bread, gallons of sassafras tea, making up silly names without meaning to, Jenna getting her ears pierced and grinning at the gold buttons in the mirror for two weeks even when her lobes swelled up like young grapes. Talking and talking, telling each other everything. (Later he realized he could have figured out Jenna's age if he'd calculated.) Crying over the abortion. God, he'd never wept like that in his life; even when they took Jenna away, he was still numb from the abortion. Sleeping on the floor. Jenna learning the piano at Bear's house. Thinking of the pain and pleasure of being two different people with that abysmal gap between selves. Jenna's parents – monsters from another universe pushing through their love with teeth and claws and a lawyer. Screaming, crying, accusations, protests. The nausea of defeat. Restraining orders. Threats. Statutory rape. Jenna's face, drained and half-dead, sick with grief that last time they saw each other across the courtroom hallway. A smuggled letter months later – 'Max, I love you. Don't change. Please wait.'

Max wiped his face and rolled another joint.

She hadn't waited. What could he really expect? Married at twenty-one, divorced at twenty-three? Someone else's wife, for shitssake.

He'd waited. No, he didn't even wait, nothing so active as that. He'd drifted. He worked for Canadian fisheries right after he lost her, then worked construction in Spokane, went back to school for a semester in L.A. He'd driven a cab in Denver, where he spent a lot of time in the mountains on his days off, getting into photography. Thousands of pictures of Georgetown and chipmunks. Before he went to Phoenix to drive a truck, he had gone back down to the old places. Kids still hung out, but the coffee houses had disco music; that radical bookstore now sold expensive turquoise jewelry. A few artisans still worked the streets, some remembered him. Remnants of the old culture stayed, but the incredible electric charge was gone. No one looked him in the face as he passed on the walk. No peace, hey brother, no you're really beautiful, man.

Business as usual.

Max was great in 1967.

If he could hold onto that, a shred of whatever it had been, and take it with him when he went down the street in the morning to find the Sage and Pepper Pottery Shop . . .

If only a lot of things. If only Sandra and Freaky and Goldie had been totally the same. He didn't know if their changes were significant, if he could extrapolate from them to Jenna. If he could sit down and draw a chart. Score Sandra high on social consciousness, which had always been her forte; Freaky on sweet affection; Goldie on the bitter intellectual edge of ethereal grace.

Jenna's tears, Jenna's smoky thoughts, falling into Jenna's mouth and hearing things that shouldn't have come from a kid. Who could have respected a 15-year-old? But she touched things and heard and saw in ways that some people never did. Frightened, but not of Max, not of Max's world. Frightened of the nasty parts of the outside world, the same things that scared the bejeezus out of Max. War, insane priorities of goods over people, bigotry, hatred, insensitivity, ignorance.

'But, why?' she asked so many times. 'Why? I don't understand why.'

And the things she loved: music, poetry, questions about what and who we are.

They held each other and listened to Watermeter's awful sitar playing in the next apartment, shared a pipe, lay in the dark and whispered onto one another's shoulder.

Then when she got sick, throwing up all the time, hardly sleeping, staring with eyebrows raised as if in Einsteinian speculation. Slender already, the girl lost fifteen pounds. Medical necessity to abort. Destroy it before it destroys Jenna. Oh, but that hurts, too. Wait. I'll get a job, feed her right, keep her in bed. Can't it be fixed? Do you have any idea how old she is? Nineteeen. Not quite. You know it's not our trip to turn runaways in, but we try to convince them that it's best to return home. She's sick, man.

Jenna?

Max, I don't want to go.

Holding a hollow girl, feeling the patchouli breeze blow through her ringlets. Sipping wine. Lighting candles. Grieving with a long look across the room.

I think I saw my brother today, watching me from his car.

God, no. God, no, Jenna.

Nightmares still of her father's face – hate, clenched fists and worry rings under his eyes. He loves her, too, but hates what she loves, loves what she hates.

Let us talk, mother, please.

You've talked enough from the looks of it. My poor child, nearly on your deathbed. He's ruined you. You'll never find a husband now.

Max, don't let them take me.

Get away from her, you fucking bastard.

Max shivered and stood, the guitar brushed the grass. He had to get his beauty sleep.

The Sage and Pepper Pottery Shop was on the west side of the street. Max stood across the street in the cool morning shadows, smoking tobacco in a pipe, nodding to a passer-by, hooking a thumb in his jeans belt loop, sometimes combing his beard with his hand. His hand trembled, but not as much as his legs.

Then there she was, walking down the street at a quarter to ten, wearing jeans and boots and a print blouse with billowing sleeves and her coffee-colored curls still magically wild. She moved with less timidity, less introspection, but it was Jenna. She unlocked the door and went inside.

Max quaked. He knocked the tobacco out of his pipe and stuffed it in his pocket. He couldn't move for a time. a confident hand turned the orange 'Closed' sign to 'Come in.'

All right.

He crossed the street, looking both ways six times because he could never remember if he saw a car or not. Taking smaller and smaller steps as he neared the door until he felt silly. He smiled involuntarily, then swallowed. Touching the latch, he depressed it just a bit, but his hand weakened.

She swept by the doorway, carrying a box. 'Didn't I unlock it?' she said easily, flinging the door open, not looking at him. Jenna's voice was richer.

He stood and looked half-heartedly around at the pots, plants, platters and prints displayed in the sunny storefront. It actually smelled vaguely of sage and pepper. Then she put her box down, looking at his face.

'I know you,' she said.

Max wavered. He knew every detail of her face; he'd sketched her memory, cherished every arrangement of atoms in her being. She saw only a lonely man standing before her with a memory focusing and unfocusing around him.

'Max?' she said tentatively.

He nodded.

'Max!' She flung her arms around him in an affectionate squeeze. He became a jellied receptacle for confusion, but recovered quickly to put his arms around her more ample waist. The patchouli breeze still wafted in her hair. He wanted to speak to her, to say, 'Jenna, Jenna, I'm back,' but he sensed that she hadn't been waiting for him to return.

'You look . . .' She hesitated. 'The same.'

'Yeah.' He chuckled and toyed with his beard. The spring of the trap that held him for years burst; he would have to move again. There she was, standing with tenderness in her eyes for something that had happened years ago to her.

He felt as though it were the next day.

'How *are* you?' she said. 'Oh, it's wonderful to see you.'

'I'm fine, just fine,' he said.

'Oh, Max.' She looked up at him. Then she turned toward the counter. 'Come and sit with me. Do you have time? Would you like some coffee?'

And he sat with her in the shop on a creaking wicker chair, sometimes touching her knee with his. Talking about old friends and marches and sit-ins and the pigs and how she'd done such-and-such and he'd learned this and about how he'd stood across from her house when he heard about Kent State because he felt so low, and how she got into her little business and didn't he get her letters? What have you been reading? Oh, yeah, I liked that too you look great it's fantastic to see you.

Jenna was still the same and yet different. Bits and pieces of what she had been fell away with time, others had been added; yet there was enough still there that he knew she still existed.

They made a date for dinner that night. She waved as he left, happily. He wandered, barely able to walk for the wonder and terror that filled him.

He paused at a store window and looked at his reflection. This is the mere passing illusion of Max, he remembered telling Goldie. What is Max?

I could have been changing, too, he thought, and still be as much Max as Jenna is Jenna, or the others are still themselves. Still regarding himself, feeling the sun grow warmer on the top of his head, he imagined his mind growing elastic again.

Change is not betrayal, he thought. That's what we fought for. Why didn't he see that before? He could talk to Jenna about that. He could do a lot of things with that idea.

/ Tuning /

I'm going to be sick, Phil thought.

He slowed the car and pulled over on the grassy shoulder. A jet roared down its flight path overhead, leaving a wake of oily vapor. He leaned his head against the steering wheel, sweat beading on his lip and hairline.

Feeling closed in, he opened the door and stood, momentarily revived by the breeze, albeit jet exhaust. He took off the pale blue cotton shirt that Pam had sent to the hospital with his belongings. It wasn't one of his; when he'd entered the emergency room, no one had considered saving the blood-soaked rag he'd worn. It annoyed him that she'd given him someone else's shirt.

Was she now telling a new lover that the clothes she *hadn't* brought belonged to her kid brother? Or the more glamorous truth: 'This ass butchered himself on my kitchen floor right where you and I made love this afternoon.'

I am angry, he thought. He got back in the car and rubbed his tired eyes. Angry, angry.

He sighed. He felt better. He was back on the road. Looking at a map, he remembered coming to this small city years ago. It had been particularly profitable, having a great many churches with out-of-tune pianos. He refolded the map and started the car again.

The old couple glanced at each other in the way that people do who've lived together a long time – unconscious of the act of reading each other's face. Phil knew that he looked bedraggled and probably untrustworthy.

'Well, it has been about five years,' the old man drawled.

The statement proved to be the answer; the screen door

opened. Phil smelled a Sunday dinner at the grandfolk's – roast beef, carrots, coffee, rolls. He followed the stout woman with thin, varicosed legs, dull grey curls, through the living room which had been lavishly furnished in the Forties. Rocking chairs, *Holiday*, *National Geographic*, and the local evening newspaper laid out on a coffee table that stood on a braided rug. A small color television was switched off, but fading ancestral photographs in gingerbread frames watched it anyway. She led him to the blond spinet.

'Would you like some coffee?' she asked.

'Yes, ma'am, I would appreciate that very much. Milk and two sugars.' He'd almost said three.

'Is half-and-half all right?'

Half-and-half. With another sugar that would be a meal. He sat down on the bench, trying not to grunt as he set his kit on the rug. 'Sounds wonderful. Thank you.'

'Mind if I watch?' Wearing a white shirt, tie, and the pants of a charcoal business suit, the old man settled into a nearby rocking chair.

'Not at all.' Phil glanced at him with a smile, fishing out his pipe and tuner. 'Been doing this so many years I don't get stage fright.'

The old man chuckled and lifted one freckled hand from the rocker and then let it down in a restless gesture. Phil guessed that they didn't have much company. 'Haven't had it tuned since our granddaughter got married. She used to come and stay with us every other weekend.'

'Oh? She move out of town?'

'Married a boy in the navy. Nice fella. They're in San Diego. We went out there last spring. She played the piano beautifully.'

'Seems to be a good little piano.' Phil twiddled a few keys and guessed that it may have been longer than five years. Definitely a friendly piano. With the number he'd seen, he had a sense about the treatment an instrument received.

Holy hell, it's hot in here.

He wiped his forehead with his sleeve. Together, he and the old man began to remove the photographs, crocheted doilies, and ceramic ballerinas from atop the piano.

'This is Wendy,' the old man said, holding up a photograph of a smiling high-school brunette.

'Pretty girl,' Phil said, shivering suddenly, as cold as if someone had opened the door to the Arctic behind him.

The old man stood over him, still holding the photograph out at arm's length.

'Excuse me . . .' Phil rose, the healing muscles wrenched across his abdomen, again the dread, deep pain, the cold sweat.

Have to get out of here. Excuse me. Not going to make it anywhere. What a disgrace. What am I going to do?

'Hey, son.' The old man put a hand on his shoulder, more weight than Phil could bear.

'I'll be all right.' He fought the dark spots blotting out the wallpaper, the man's brow, wobbling and moving unsteadily. Sitting abruptly, he put his head between his knees.

Hurts like hell, *like hell*, damnit.

He saw the piano tuner slip out of his fingers and thud on the rug between his shoes.

Phil had sat near the casket at old Tackett's funeral. Funny how old people get so small and dry. Tackett wore his Sunday 'concert suit', his hands folded. Those hands had been full of music once, reaching an octave and two notes. Now they looked frail and brittle, his neatly pared fingernails blueish. Still. Dead.

Called away from college in a distant state, Phil had felt even more like a foreigner in his home town than before. He knew his role of oddball, and it was compounded by the college-boy image. He was more surly and distant than before, maybe because they expected it. He didn't even look toward the congregation as he waited for his cue to play. The smell of gladioli and chrysanthemums and ladies' perfume in the damp heat smothered any hope of a clean breath. Looking at their funereal faces would not have made him more comfortable.

The preacher turned from the altar. Phil stiffened and for a moment his hands hesitated over the keys. He had to get it right. Old Tackett deserved at least that.

First, Debussy's 'Claire de Lune.'

'Have I told you the story,' Tackett had once said, 'about the man who was so moved by this music that when he decided to end his life, he sat by his record player and, at the last note, shot himself?'

'Yes, sir. It's depressing.'

'Oh, don't you worry, Phil. You're not the sort that will ever need to do that. You've got genius. You're not only our next Paderewski, or Horowitz, but a new Chopin.'

Then, Beethoven's 'Für Elise.'

Phil remembered a quiet day, just before he left for college. Tackett leaning on his elbow on the scores stacked on the lamp table, smoking an unfiltered cigarette. He didn't comment on the composition that Phil had finally brought out of hiding. Phil swung his legs around on the piano bench and faced his teacher. 'Well?'

Tackett seemed distant. 'Before I critique that aggravating concoction you've just played, let me tell you that simplicity is not a fault. Isn't 'Für Elise' beautiful and yet simple?'

No one applauded at the end of the peculiar funeral music. They sat stiffly in their hard pews, blinking, slapping at the flies that swarmed through the open door. Probably relieved that the esoteric thunder was over, they waited for the preacher to finish so they could get back to Saturday afternoon watermelon, radio, croquet. They probably thought it was damned inconsiderate of old Tackett to get buried on a weekend. Even now they whispered about whether to go to Sally's Dinette or just home for hot dogs.

Phil finally looked across the altar, across the end of the casket, first at Katie, who dabbed her eyes, then at Mrs

Tackett. She turned her head slightly, refocusing her eyes; she smiled at him. Just a little. Just enough.

She probably still believed what Tackett had always said: 'Someday people are going to ask you who your teacher was. If you mention my name, that will be the achievement of my life.'

Skinny, shy Philip Benson had carried the sum of another man's life in his fingers. It wasn't until years later that Phil realized the mawkish sentimentality and self-delusion that Tackett had been infected with . . . and had infected Phil with as well.

Phil propped himself up on one elbow and took another swallow of coffee. 'I'm feeling a lot better.'

Mrs Johnston, perched on the edge of a wooden chair, smiled with solicitous satisfaction. 'Why don't you stay for dinner? It'll be ready in half an hour.'

'I don't have the strength to refuse, ma'am.'

'Had an appendectomy myself,' Mr Johnston said, still lingering on the earlier conversation. 'Long time ago. They were experimenting with a new drug – sulfa. Saved my life. I was ruptured.' Again, the nervous raising of his old hand, but this time it dropped to his knee. 'Had less trouble than when Mother had her gall bladder out. All those new anti-bi-otics.'

Mrs Johnston frowned. 'All right now. The nurses said that gall bladder is worse than appendix anyway. He doesn't pay a bit of attention,' she said to Phil.

'Was ruptured,' Mr Johnston repeated, nodding.

'So you were,' she said, plainly unimpressed.

Phil sat upright, then leaned back against the sofa cushions.

'You're still awfully pale,' she said. 'I knew you weren't feeling right when you came to our door.'

'That's the way with county hospitals, they send you out too soon if you can't pay,' Mr Johnston said.

Mrs Johnston rose to chase a buzzer in the kitchen. In a

momentary loss for conversation, Mr Johnston said, 'Time for the news.'

They watched the world going to hell on a color screen: civil wars, terrorists, anonymous murders without motives, the economy. He felt guilty because he thought he should care more, but it seemed so distant from the cozy little house. The death agonies of modern civilization gnawed at his healing incision.

I have to live through it, he thought simply.

He heard Mrs Johnston opening and shutting the oven, stirring saucepans, getting things out of the cupboard. Ordinarily, he would join her. Helping out in strange kitchens made him feel as though he belonged somewhere.

'Dinner!' she sang from the kitchen. At last.

What a feast after hospital food – pot roast, carrot and raisin salad, orange juice, milk, coffee, asparagus, whole wheat rolls. He enjoyed it as much as if it were Szechwan Duck.

'How long have you been tuning pianos?' Mr Johnston asked.

'Oh, about fifteen years. Sometimes I have jobs actually playing the piano, too. Just finished a job playing for a small theatre group.' Or did it finish me?

'You travel around a lot then?'

'Mmm.' He nodded, his mouth full of buttered roll.

'Never been married?' Mrs Johnston asked.

'Mmm-mm.' He shook his head.

Why did he think of Katie every time someone asked him that? Katie who had twice been someone else's wife and never his own. Katie at sixteen, violin tucked under her chin, funny glasses sliding down her nose; Katie at eighteen, telling him to go away and have a career because everyone had told them that they had to sacrifice for the glorious artistry of Phil Benson; Katie at twenty-eight, six months pregnant, this time Louis's; Katie at thirty-two shouting at her eldest not to run over the hose with the lawnmower.

I should become a Buddhist monk. Renounce the world mentally if I can't quite renounce it physically. Steep in thoughts of The Universe, eat sticky rice and sip green tea. Chopin wasted his time in bedrooms, I waste mine in a car. Need to change . . .

'What's the matter?' Mrs Johnston asked.

Phil realized that he was musing rather than eating. Only a little food had assuaged what he'd thought was a raging appetite. He stared into the carrots. 'This is wonderful food, but . . .'

'Why don't you go upstairs and take a nap?'

'I could use a nap,' he said.

He followed her up into a garrett-like bedroom with a window in the eaves, complete with a window seat. She'd barely turned the light on before he was stretched out. Must be granddaughter Wendy's room, he thought vaguely, as Mrs Johnston shook the quilt over him.

Pam had found him in the coffee shop after their argument. Accepting her presence across the table, he watched her practice her art. Now she played the part of a contrite lover. He'd seen the expression many times from below stage where he plunked out God-awful tunes for God-awful plays. But Pamela was a brilliant actress. He thought she might be sincere.

The waitress brought Pam a menu and poured Phil another cup of coffee. He stirred the heavy spoon, clink-clink, against the mug.

'I think I need help,' she said. Ivory face, ebony hair, mahogany eyes. Mediterranean sublime.

Phil waited, lighting a cigarette.

'I'm afraid of what I might do someday. You know. I could easily kill someone. You, maybe. But I don't know why. Sometimes I just hate.' She showed her teeth in a grimacing smile. 'I hate you because you don't need me. You'd leave me in a minute, wouldn't you?'

'I haven't.' But he didn't tell her how close he'd come only an hour ago.

'I like to see that people are as weak as I am. It really gripes me when you're a goody-goody because I know it's not true. I know why you were upset about that stupid playwright the other night. She treated you like a common stagehand. Not like an artist, a genius.' She put her hand over her heart melodramatically. 'You were not appreciated.' Then she glared at him. 'That's not my fault.'

Phil nodded. 'I'm sorry I took it out on you.'

She took his hand and he returned a half-hearted grasp. 'I hate sterling examples of humanity without a single bruise on their selfless egos. I like rotten, mean people. That's why I like you.'

Phil laughed.

Pam smiled, then shrugged. 'You're a real bag of snakes, aren't you? And they all eat you up instead of other people. I know you're talented but it's all a waste.'

'I'm thirty-eight . . .' he said.

'And waiting. What is that under the bed? You think somebody's going to come along and publish all those moldy compositions once you're dead or something? That stupid letter!' She laughed loudly enough that others in the café glanced her way.

Phil was embarrassed. He'd never expected anyone to go looking through his things. He still hadn't gotten the hang of living with another person.

'It's never going to happen to you, Phil. You're never going to blaze up to the forefront of American music. You don't even have an agent. You don't hang around with the right people. And if you did, you'd treat them with that purist attitude of yours and not play their games, anyway. Oh, the suffering artist.'

'Look, I apologized. You don't need to do this any more.'

'You're self-centered and naïve. And *old*. And I hate your stupid, syrupy music.'

'Enough,' he said.

'It's true that Elgin didn't know what she was dealing with,' she went on, taking a burning gulp of coffee. 'But to all the world except yourself, you're a total zero.'

Phil leaned back in the booth and regarded her smile. 'You have all manner of guns, sweetie.'

Pamela grinned. 'Truth. Ouch?'

He woke up hearing the doves' rippling voices as they strutted the rooftop. He rolled over slowly and watched their grey-brown feathers catch the sunlight dully. A nice day. Sunny, Indian summer. The leaves had mostly turned, a gaudy display of brown and yellow fluttered toward the rain gutters.

Autumn. Like me. He pushed himself upright and found himself eye to eye with his own face in the mirror of a frilly vanity. Or was that his face? The last time he'd seen his reflection . . . that last day at Pam's before he stuck a greasy kitchen knife into his guts. Entranced by a candle's ephemeral beauty, he'd expected a peaceful transition into nothingness.

Instead he had pain, then the hospital, and now this.

He was shocked at his appearance. So thin, and even more grey hairs, he looked at least fifteen years older than he felt he should.

He held his hands in front of him. Long fingers, square palms, hairy and strong. He could have been a good carpenter, or typesetter, or weaver. Why did he have to be a mediocre musician? He was a drifter and meant nothing to anyone – except his old friend Katie, who would have missed him if he'd run that knife a little further in and pulled it across.

'I'm tired,' he said aloud to the sunny room with the patchwork quilt and Winslow Homer prints. He knew he could stop and rest. Perhaps even here, as a boarder.

He would suffocate.

The Johnstons, the Wantabors, the Yangs . . . Old people he'd known, sitting at home, living their final days in a quiescence that Phil knew he could never personally tolerate, but that was soothing for him for the times that they took him in, fed him, listened to his stories and music. Quite a few were decent pianists themselves, others retired music teachers, eager to talk about and teach more. He learned from them and cared about them, considering some of the evenings spent with them the finest in his life.

But he needed new air, new faces, possibilities, and hope.

Wanderlust? he wondered, swinging his feet carefully onto the floor.

Tackett had always said that the best warm-up was Bach, because it took precision. Never warm up with sentiment. After weeks without practice, his hands seemed stiff but he played on. Mrs Johnston brought the coffee; Mr Johnston sat nearby. Now, they remained appreciative as he played on through a Brandenburg, Brahms' Hungarian Dances, the first movement of the 'Emperor', and Rachmaninov preludes.

When his thirst was abated, he wondered if he'd made them weary. He looked and saw a kind of affection in Mrs Johnston's eyes.

'We were wondering,' she said, 'if you wanted to stay for a few days and then . . .'

Phil would have done anything for those eyes.

The Association of Retired People met in the basement of an 105-year-old church. He watched them file in, gathering in groups, smiling uncertain, toothy smiles. They fidgeted, holding handbags or hats in their liver-spotted hands.

Phil sat in a corner, drinking weak tea and smoking a cigarette. He listened as a jolly man with a polished manner, almost a show-biz personality, cited the dues situation. A few dragged out dollars and change from their pockets and egg-shaped moneyholders. They talked about appointing representatives to visit members in the hospital.

'But, Charley, I went last week and he doesn't even recognize anyone.'

'Now, Jennie, you know that sometimes people understand more than they let on. I think we should still visit.'

'Then somebody else go,' Jennie said and 300 pounds sat with an air of final decision.

'All right.'

'I'll go,' another voice said. 'My cousin's in for her heart again anyway.'

'Again!'

'Oh, you know . . .'

The president of the club interrupted. 'Listen, now that all the business has been settled. The Johnstons have brought us a guest tonight.'

'A what?' someone asked, aside.

'A guest.'

Phil took some pleasure in the fact that most of them looked his way. He had been toying with the idea that he seemed old enough to be a member now, but obviously he looked like an outsider.

'This man has been touring the country as a pianist for seventeen years, playing in so many places we can't even list them all.' The president turned and motioned to Phil. 'Ladies and gentlemen, Mr Philip Benson.'

Phil rose self-consciously from his corner and walked to the old upright where they had placed it – approximately center stage on a painted concrete floor. Fortunately, he'd come early with his pitch pipe and tuned it. He hoped the choirmaster would appreciate it for a few days.

He started slowly with Schumann, then some Mozart, quiet and short pieces. Then his own transcriptions of a Vivaldi flute concerto. There were a few coughs and shuffles as he played, and at first polite applause between.

They listened.

They warmed up and he warmed up. Each piece brought more enthusiasm, and he began to hear 'wonderful' being murmured under the applause.

This was not playing background music for a two-bit drama, or an all-you-can-eat cafeteria, or smoky lounge. They slapped those bony hands together and looked sideways at each other with smiles. Listened to Bach's Italian Concerto as if every note reduced their time in purgatory.

He worked hard for them. His hands touched the keys with deftness and feeling, Philip Benson in tails and leather shoes, hot spotlights and a duchess in the audience.

Oh, God, what I might have been . . .

But he didn't play that bitterness for them. He touched other untouched places. He held the last note a little too long, lingering.

He turned to them.

Carnegie Hall dissolved into the basement of an old church. Fragile people in folding chairs clapped, elbows jutting. One woman, tears in her eyes, stood. The man next to her rose, leaning on his cane. Then another, and another, and another. Eagerness, life – years upon years of life – charged through them as they got to their feet, still applauding him. A man in a wheelchair rolled forward and held his hands as high as he could because he couldn't stand with the others.

He saw the gnarled faces and wispy hair over freckled brows. He knew he'd done something right and it bewildered him. No audience, not even at Carnegie, could have touched him more. Breathless with gratitude, he felt some strange thing. He had forgotten that he had to prove to them, he had only given, very simply, because they asked.

'Play another, Mr Benson!'

Mr Benson! Only thirty-eight years old, while Agatha, Harry, and Ida are all seventy-plus. He trembled, fearing tears, fearing so much that it would break him. He sat down at the piano once more.

He played the Katherine Sonata by Benson. Simple, from the first gentle notes to the last sweep.

And there's more, he thought. There's even more in me than this.

/ The Window Jesus /

Joe and Velma lived for twenty-three years on their farm. They grew sorghum and vegetables, had some chickens, and a milk goat. Joe sometimes made glass in the shed where his father, too, had learned to dabble in the art.

Velma, a religious woman, mostly took care of the house and garden.

At supper, she bowed her head and prayed for the Lord personally to bless the food sitting on their table, asking Him to keep up their good health. At night, she prayed again.

One evening, she read about a woman seeing Jesus in her screen door. Velma thought that was unfairly partial of the Lord. She thought she deserved a sign, too. 'He knows I say my prayers good and regular.'

Joe didn't know much about this kind of thing. It was true that Velma was a good person. She baked and canned for the church; she gave eggs to the poor. She made quilts for families who had fires or floods or unexpected deaths. Sure, sometimes she got a little testy, but it tried her patience that others weren't as good as she was.

Joe thought it was possible that the Lord would think enough of her to say howdy.

One day as he worked in the glassmaking shed, he remembered an article he'd read in his trade magazine about putting subtle images in glass. Called 'ghost glass', it only worked in certain lights at certain angles.

The first time she saw the new window in their bedroom, the light wasn't right. 'Why did you make a new window?' she asked.

'The other one rattled,' Joe said. 'Didn't fit right.' He could hardly wait until she saw her 'ghost'.

She shrugged; he knew more about these things, just as she knew more about tomato worms and measuring for drapes.

Eight or nine days passed, the weather began to change. The September moon got rounder and heavier as it sailed over their land.

Velma kneeled beside the bed, just as she had done since her mother had persuaded her little knees to the floor. She prayed for Joe, she prayed for her church friends, and all the people who lived in town. She told God how good things were down here, no matter what the news report said.

She lifted her head and saw Jesus in the window.

'Oh, Lordy,' Velma said. 'Here it is, here's my sign.'

Joe sat down on the other side of the bed. The full moon was just the right angle and brightness to show off those marks he'd so painstakingly scratched into the glass.

'Do you see it, Joe?'

'Do you like it?' he asked.

'You don't see what I see, do you?' Her voice was soft.

'Sure.' Joe pointed. 'I made that window. It's the best I could do because I didn't know how to put . . .'

'Joseph.'

He hadn't known how to put Jesus in the screen door, which he'd felt Velma deserved as well as anyone else in the world.

'You may have made that window, but God put that poor suffering face in there.' She gazed across the calico quilt at it.

Joe shrugged. He knew that she liked it and that was the important thing. If she wanted it to be her miracle, he knew he couldn't talk her out of it.

The next day three of the women from church sat in the kitchen with Velma, each with one hand in their lap and the other on the table. Mugs of coffee cooled before them.

Velma looked pale. 'I know it was there. I saw it last night as I said my prayers. Joe saw it, too.' By the flatness of her voice, he figured she'd said those words about twenty times already.

The ladies looked at one another, then at Velma.

Velma noticed that Joe had come into the kitchen. 'It's gone,' she said.

Joe patted her shoulder. 'Maybe it'll come back tonight.'

She sighed. 'Well, I suppose it was the experience of my life, whether I see it again or not.' But she looked sadly at the table as she brushed the crumbs with her finger.

On her knees, Velma saw it again that night. The next evening, the three ladies and their husbands came for raisin pie and ice-cream after dinner and saw the moon rise up over Jesus's shoulder. They saw the wreath of thorns and downturned mouth.

Viewing it more critically because strangers were looking at it, Joe noticed that the angle of the nose was all wrong. He was better at tracing than drawing. But no one seemed to care.

By the next week, just about the whole town had stood in Joe and Velma's bedroom one night or another. Some took pictures which didn't show anything, making it even more mysterious.

But the course and size of the moon changed until the face disappeared back into the pane of glass.

Velma baked strawberry pie, apple cake, and cheese logs for all the visitors who still dropped by about the time of the weather report. Dutifully, they stood and waited for Jesus in the window, but he'd stopped coming.

Velma didn't care. She knew now for sure that God was paying attention to all those extra quilts and pots of chilli she made for other folks. She radiated. She was kinder and more forgiving, even to those in the eastside church.

Joe worried. He knew he'd tried to tell her what he'd done, but she didn't want to hear it. He wanted to talk about it with her, but she seemed as happy as an unofficial saint. She laughed and hugged his neck the way she used to when he'd first brought her to the farm. He liked that. He liked remembering the days when he could hardly wait to get in from the fields.

Almost a month after that first night, a man came by from an out-of-state newspaper. He'd heard about the face in the window. This was Velma's chance to be in history with the Screen Door Jesus, the Tortilla Jesus, maybe even the Shroud of Turin.

As soon as the broad moon hit the window pane the newspaper man saw the face, too. He had a camera that could take pictures without flash cubes if he set it right, so he took pictures. He also took pictures of Velma in her blue cotton robe, kneeling at her prayers, facing the Window Jesus. He took pictures of Joe and Velma on their sofa. He took pictures of the farm, but never asked about the shed where Joe made the glass.

The reporter went back to his city and wrote about it, sending a copy of the story when it came out in his newspaper. It showed up in other newspapers, too. Velma started making pies and snacks again. People came from all over the state, then from across the country. A woman came all the way from Sweden.

Then a man showed up with a movie camera. He wasn't as friendly as the others, he didn't nod and smile. He looked at everything carefully. Poking around the glass-making shed, he read the magazines, too. He asked Joe in front of Velma (with the camera and a bright light turned on their shoulders) if he'd made the pane of glass.

Joe fought. He was a good man. He didn't know how to be anything else, but this lie had started to twist around inside him like a terrible snake. He croaked when he answered, 'Yes.' And the newsman made him say it again, just as if he were a kid and the newsman were his father.

'Yes, I made the glass and I put the face in it. It was a present for Velma.'

Joe didn't even look at Velma. He walked away. He thought about all the people in town saying things that weren't nice to Velma if they found out, and Velma being disappointed and mad at him. He wished he'd never made it, or even heard of 'ghost glass.'

Joe was depressed. He walked through his sorghum with his hands in his pockets.

He watched the van with the man and the movie camera drive away later in the afternoon, and Velma stood, shading her eyes with her hand, watching them go.

Finally, he went in for dinner. Velma seemed as cheerful as ever. She said her grace, blessing everyone as usual. Then she said, 'Bless all those hypocrite non-believers, too,' and passed Joe the roast chicken.

/ River Baby /

Maxine opened the apartment door and looked down the concrete walkway, bright in the hot sun, for her daughter. Angela squatted by the rusted rail, placidly watching a river of pee flowing between her spread feet.

'What the hell are you doing?' Maxine jerked her daughter's arm and dragged her in the door. Surprised, the 3-year-old couldn't stop midstream. As Angela's legs dangled against her, Maxine felt the warm pee splashing on her.

Maxine fought Angela into the bathroom. The kid screeched as Maxine lifted the toilet lid. 'You're going to hell,' she said confidently, shoving Angela's face into the water.

Angela bobbed up, gurgling.

Maxine pushed her face down once more for good measure, just in case once didn't teach her. 'Take a bath,' she said over Angela's moist wail, turning on the bath faucets.

Maxine stood at the mirror while Angela clambered obediently into the tub, sniffling. Occasionally, she gave a sob.

Maxine combed her short hair, which was like the way Elvis Presley had worn his hair. She'd kept her hair long when Tony was around. It had been soft and shining, layered and curly, the color of brown sugar. That was before the kid came along. It had been easy to spend an hour or two on her hair and face just in order to go shopping or to work.

What for? She slapped the comb down. Men were just a bunch of trouble anyway; she'd spent all that time to get one, but it only caused her grief. They always want what they don't get, just like Dad. She smirked at her reflection. Her mother hadn't put up with much from Dad, though. Whenever he'd come sneaking around full of apologies and sweet words, Mama had attacked, sometimes knee first. Mama had balls, for a woman.

Maxine felt a drop of water on her leg. She looked over at Angela. 'Don't you splash me again,' she warned.

Her mama had been tough, but she never said the f-word. Sometimes when Maxine let f-words slip out, she looked over her shoulder, just in case her mother had taken that moment to make a surprise visit.

Angela had turned her attention to her hands underwater. Her dark hair pointed down her back. A ring of green and yellow bruises colored her hip like a tattooed wreath. She was a small child, with big, dark eyes like her father's. Those eyes meant nothing but trouble to Maxine. They didn't melt her heart at all.

'I hope you don't turn out mean and hateful like your father,' Maxine said to Angela. 'You look just like 'im sometimes.'

Angela looked up at her mother briefly, then began to wash with a bar of soap too big for her hands. Her fingers slipped and readjusted around the edges of it. She cocked her head this way and that, half-singing, half-humming a little song under her breath.

'What are you singing?' Maxine asked.

'Nothing,' Angela said.

'What? Tell me.'

'Nothing.'

'You're a little smarty ass, aren't you?' Maxine said, moving toward her daughter. 'What were you singing?'

'Mommy, nothing, nothing, Mommy!' And then she began to cry, looking – not at Maxine's face, but – at the hands outstretched toward her.

'What. Were. You. Singing?' Maxine pounded her fists on the edge of the tub.

*'Where. Were. You?' Maxine had asked Tony. She hadn't seen
him in three days. Hey, they weren't married, but didn't they
have a kid together? And didn't his mother make him promise to
take care of her? He had said he loved her in front of his whole
family. How long had it been since he'd kissed her more than
just a quick one on the way out or as he came home at night? She
knew he'd been with someone else. She could smell someone else
on his fingers, some other woman's shampoo in his hair. They'd
probably taken showers together and everything. Maxine hated,
loved Tony. She felt him slipping away and didn't want him to
go but everything about him irritated her. Here she was with the
goddamn bawling baby who needed to be taken care of all the
time (except when Maxine left her to go sit with a neighbor or
run down to the grocery). And she looked in Tony's eyes and saw
the insolence because he didn't care any more. 'Go screw
yourself,' he said, and she put her raging hands around his
throat because he was so evil and hateful and had done her so
wrong. She wanted to make him sputter and turn purple
and die, but he knocked her down and she never saw him
again.*

Angela looked back at Maxine with wet eyes that had the
fear taken out of them suddenly. Her little baby mouth was
firm. 'I wish Daddy would come back and kill you,' she
said.

That's when Maxine did it.

She sat on the toilet lid for a long time, legs crossed. She
just stared at the door of the cabinet.

She went into the living room and got a cigarette out of
her purse. Then she sat with it in her hand feeling like she
was in a dream. 'Jesus,' she said aloud, shaking. Then she
lit her cigarette.

Not thinking about anything in particular, she smoked.
Vague impressions of packing, disposing of what was in the
bathtub fluttered through her mind, but her deeper concentration was on how much money she had in her check book,

when payday was coming up, were her favorite jeans washed and such.

Payday would come the day after tomorrow.

She had to wait.

She went into the bathroom and looked down into the tub. Angela's eyes were open and staring up through the water, but once Maxine had pulled her lids down, the thing in the bottom of the tub didn't seem so real. It felt like a horrible big doll made of blue-white fish flesh, clammy and rubbery. Still and silent, it wasn't the brat any more. Her hair had all settled to the bottom of the tub and didn't move.

Maxine flipped the drain open and the water began to suck away from the thing in the tub and down the drain. Soap scum stuck in a line to the chubby legs.

She picked up her purse and left the apartment with the windows open. It was still too early in the spring to turn the air-conditioning on. She drove to a bar out at the north end of town. Those fluffy, sincere kids that hung out in the bars near campus annoyed her. She liked the whiskey-voiced, the silent drinkers, the men who didn't expect you to talk about much, just have a good time. Those were real people.

She sat in a booth and drank beer and a shot or two. Though she hated to, she bought the expensive cigarettes out of the machine. The barmaid came and refilled her drink and emptied the ashtray, but no one else came to her table. She felt bitchy. She didn't really want to talk to anyone, but wondered why no one came over. I'm a mess, she thought, running her hand through her hair. Since Tony had gone, she'd put on fifteen pounds, stopped wearing make-up. Why the hell should she worry about her looks? Men were pus. Unless she could just find a rich one, one who was nice, too. He wouldn't even have to be handsome. Just nice. Maybe have a trailer, so they could go traveling across the country.

Maxine spotted a guy at the bar who looked as if he had a

lot of money. She smiled at him, but he shifted his look as if he hadn't seen her.

I would have been a better mother if I hadn't had to worry about clothes and electric bills. Worrying about money makes a person sick and tired, and it's so easy to holler at a kid when you feel that way. Like Mama. Mama loved us but she had all those troubles. Maxine had never understood that when she was younger. Now she did, and suddenly she yearned to tell her mother how she understood. She missed her mama and her eyes filled with tears; she pretended it was the smoke, blinking and wiping with the back of her wrist instead of her fingers.

When the bar closed, she drove out west where the big houses were. She parked in front of a huge red house that had six windows facing the street, one of them a bay. She lit a cigarette and leaned back in her car seat looking at those windows and wishing that she'd met a rich man who could buy her a house like that, and she fell asleep.

She called in sick to work from the pancake house, where she polished off the breakfast special and lingered over coffee. It was a windy day and that made her feel low. The gusts were so strong, even the sunlight was white instead of yellow under fast-moving clouds, as if the wind had whipped the color out. Pale foreheads showed as people walked against the wind; clothes clung to thighs. Street lights swayed, bags and paper tumbled across intersections under the wheels of cars.

Maxine stared out of the windows of the pancake house and drank her fourth cup of coffee. She didn't know what to do, where to go. Every time she thought about going down to Houston to see her mother, she got nervous.

Everything had gone dry and tasteless and ruined. Just like after smelling burnt popcorn, you don't want to eat popcorn; people seemed charred and ugly. Maxine's eyes viewed the scene in front of her without interest.

She thought of her sister, Jewell, who lived down on the coast with her husband, Clifford. Jewell and Maxine had never been close, but Maxine decided she could go there until she resolved what to do.

She managed to kill the day window shopping. At dusk, she returned to the apartment. There was a strange, icky smell when she opened the door.

'Pooey,' she said.

But she got used to the smell. She made a pot of coffee and sat down and smoked in the dark, the way she used to in her bedroom when she was in junior high school. She didn't want to move.

I've really messed things up, she thought. The apartment was so quiet. Even knowing that she could go out again, she didn't want to leave. It got windier and windier outside, rattling the windows, but without rain.

She lay on the living room floor and watched television. She had to fight to stay awake, even during the interesting parts of an old Burt Reynolds movie. She finally got up and washed her face.

The bathroom smelled the worst. As she brushed her teeth, she couldn't even look in the mirror because she had a feeling that the thing in the bathtub was sitting up and staring at her, even though she knew it couldn't be true. It lay silently in the bottom of the tub.

She packed most of her clothes, her favorite cosmetics and just a few extras and took them down to the car. When she came back in, she looked around the apartment with her hands on her hips.

She spread a blanket on the bathroom floor. Then she thought that she didn't really want to touch the thing that had been Angela. With the blanket wrapped around her arms, she leaned over and pulled on the arms of the thing.

Heart thumping, she recoiled. Bodies are supposed to be stiff and this one wasn't.

Angela was alive.

She stood up with her breath in her mouth, waiting for the kid to rise up and say something smart. How had she made that awful smell and stayed so still for all this time?

She looked at her. She was dead, all right. Maxine didn't want to touch it any more. Maybe I could spread blood all over the apartment and leave her, then they would think I was dead, too . . .

No. She had to ditch the kid.

She didn't know why it wasn't stiff, but she knew no one was at home behind that face. Nothing could live and be that color or smell like that. She picked it up, as if it were sleepy Angela in the back seat after a drive-in movie. The second time wasn't so awful, knowing what to expect. She felt as if her fingers, even padded by the blanket, were sinking into the putrid flesh, but she didn't check it out.

She carried her swaddled child down to the car and closed all the doors very quietly. Sitting in the driver's seat, she paused with her hand on the key and then decided to roll the windows down.

It didn't take her long to get down to Town Lake, but she drove for a while, trying to find the best place. The wind still blew. The trees were hoarse, the grass black, and the river blacker. No one was on the street in the wind.

As she carried the burden down to the river, she started to think about how bodies float. If Angela floated now, she would have been better off leaving her in the tub. So she went to the car and looked in the trunk.

Tony' tool chest. That damned tool chest. They'd had one hell of a fight over it in K-Mart one day because Maxine wanted a slow cooker and Tony wanted a new tool chest. They couldn't have both. He won and when her next birthday came around, she still didn't get a slow cooker. Even in the summer, she had to turn on the stove to make supper.

She loaded everything into the tool chest that was heavy and small, wrapped a rope around the handle and then tied it all around the blanket.

She scanned the banks. Although she couldn't hear

anyone because of the wind, she felt that someone stood near her. The wind made it quiet in a way because there were no traffic sounds, no sirens or city noise, only the soft sounds of the trees and the river licking the concrete shores.

She carried everything down to a point just beyond the bridge. It was weedy here; no one picnicked in this spot when they could lie on the neat lawn further down the shore.

She tossed the thing that had been her daughter, the blanket, and the tool chest in where the water looked deepest. They disappeared.

Once she'd gotten her paycheck and cashed it, driven away from the windstorm and into the daylight, Maxine started thinking about Jewell. Her sister had always gotten the better of everything. Even her name was better. Jewell had been Mama's favorite, if Mama had favorites, if she'd ever been sober enough to notice her kids. Maxine had always been a little on the chubby side and brown-haired, but Jewell had been a strawberry blonde with long, tapering fingers that looked good with any color nail polish.

Once she had passed San Antonio and headed for the flat farmland near the coast, Maxine lost the feeling that she had no place to go to but Jewell's. She could always work something out somehow, even if she had to sleep in her car. She didn't feel as spooked during the day. Going to Jewell's didn't seem so urgent.

But she drove on to her sister's anyway. It would be easiest. As she ate breakfast in a truck stop café because it was still too early to arrive, she watched the waitress and cook listening to the morning news on a small black and white TV at the end of the counter. She wondered if anyone knew yet. She pictured herself as in a movie, seeing a report of her crime on the television.

Nothing. How would they know? No one ever would, unless they found the thing in the lake.

She drove past Jewell and Clifford's house at regular

speed the first time, just to see if they were home. Not only was Cliff's old red pickup sitting out front, but there was Jewell's big yellow car that she drove back and forth to her job at the fabric store.

The second time around the block, she pulled up in front of the truck and walked up to the low brick house. A palm tree grew right out of the front yard, an ugly tree, dead on top. People grew them down here, just because they could, not because they were nice trees.

Jewell answered the door. 'Maxine,' she said, 'What on earth are you doing here?'

'Just come for a visit. Baby's at her grandmother's.' Maxine knew that she didn't sound convincingly social, but Jewell didn't seem to notice. She put one arm around Maxine lightly, as if she had grease on her hands.

'Clifford's just about to leave for work. Come on in, sit down. Cliff! Maxine's here,' she called toward the bedroom.

Clifford came out. He was huge in the belly, hair grey and thin on his head, and had a shy smile. 'Hello!' he said, bravely.

'Well, I'm sorry for busting in so early,' Maxine said. But she couldn't think of an excuse. She tried to invent a way to leave again. They were thinking about how much money she wanted from them. Being in Jewell's house irritated and depressed her. It was fluffy and clean. It had no balls.

'Would you like some coffee?' Jewell asked.

'Sure.' She went to the bathroom and washed, feeling gritty from the drive. When she came out, Cliff had just gotten into his truck and was driving away. Jewell stood at the window and waved bye-bye to him.

Maxine hated him and his wheezing, overweight shyness. And she hated Jewell as she stood there, her fingers working at the cuffs of her frilly blouse, at her watch, then poking into her curled hair sprayed so thick it was like dew on a spider's web.

Jewell looked at her the way she used to when Mama

would leave Maxine and her alone, like now what am I going to do with you? Jewell always had some way of straightening Maxine out, like putting her on mock trial and carrying out a sentence of hanging, all but kicking the chair out, or just slapping her around every time she moved.

Maxine wanted to leave. 'I guess I shouldn't have busted in like this,' she said and picked up her purse from the end of the sofa.

'No stay! Don't be silly. We haven't talked in *ages*.' Jewell took her fingers out of her hair and looked Maxine straight in the eye. 'Let me get your coffee.'

Maxine sat down, sullen, trapped. Jewell returned with the cups hooked in her long, manicured index fingers and a skein of yarn squashed under her arm.

'Now. Tell me how Angela is doing,' Jewell said. She settled down in the chair farthest in the room from Maxine. Maxine sipped her coffee, feeling almost drugged, she was so sleepy.

'Fine.'

Jewell began to knit. The aluminum needles were like dull green neon lights shining through a variegated beige, orange and brown yarn. They made a soft sliding sound.

Maxine rubbed her eyes and tried to keep them open.

Pulling more yarn from the skein in forward jerks, Jewell said, 'I saw Mama last month.'

Maxine wondered who went to see whom. 'Oh. How is she?'

'Fine.'

Maxine turned her face away and yawned. She could take a nap on the sofa as soon as Jewell left for work. Might be a few things she could borrow and pawn till she got settled somewhere. Maxine daydreamed about getting a job, maybe in a nice restaurant, where she could meet a retired naval officer or something, and they could get married and she could live in a house on the coast. Those military guys could still be young and fun even when they retired . . .

'You know how Mama used to beat us?' Jewell was saying, as if remembering an annual outing to the fairgrounds. It was like a memory that's been handled and recalled so much it's worn and soft.

'What?' Maxine yawned again.

'She feels real sorry about it sometimes. She talked about you, you know. And how sweet little Angela is, so you don't get the urge to beat her like Mama did us.'

Maxine felt a little more awake. 'I'd like to know how people keep kids without a thump every now and then,' she said, her scorn covering a quavering in her voice.

'Some can,' Jewell said.

'So what?' Maxine drank more coffee. How long was she going to sit here and put up with Jewell? Why did she come here? Jewell was so damned perfect. Mama said this, Mama said that. Making it sound like she and Mama were so much smarter.

She pictured Jewell in the bathtub – her hair still lacquered into the same curls even underwater, and even though her mouth was opening and closing and bubbles came out with funny round screams in them.

Maxine felt faint. Her blood all seemed to leave her body. It felt like Mama watched her think about Jewell drowning.

Jewell's knitting needles made the same slick sounds over and over again as she talked into the pattern that the yarn made. 'I still never could talk to Mama about things, though, Maxine.'

When Jewell sighed, Maxine stared at her.

'When Cliff and I were married about a year, he wanted to have his kids from Shirley for the summer. You know 'em. They were at the big reunion that Fourth when y'all came down. Remember?'

Maxine shrugged.

'Well, I thought I liked those kids, but I started to chase after them when Cliff was gone. Then I started to holler. I'm sure the neighbors could hear it all. Maxine, you shoulda heard – I sounded just like Mama. And then I started spanking them, every day. They made noise, they ate the wrong things out of the refrigerator, they broke stuff, and walked in the tomatoes. Oh, Lord, they seemed so *bad* to me. Little devils.'

So? Maxine wondered, crossing her arms over her chest.

Jewell's hands paused for just a moment, like humming birds settled. But they trembled. Jewell looked at Maxine. 'I beat one of those little boys until he was black and blue and still that wasn't enough. I couldn't stop.'

Maxine waited. Knitting again, Jewell didn't say any more. 'Well, what then?' she asked.

Jewell looked up. 'I went to a therapist. Cliff made me go because his son told him how crazy I got. The doctor said it was a sickness I got from Mama. She never beat you the way she beat me.' Jewell's voice got higher and thinner.

Maxine watched her sister's hand moving, moving. Mama's hands moved like that, always picking, shaping, scratching, sliding, drumming.

Jewell's face screwed up. 'Cliff's been so good to me,' she said, squeaking now. She let out a big breath. 'The therapist said it would be best if we took the kids in every now and then, a weekend every month or so.' She stopped knitting and put her hands, needles, yarn and all to her forehead. Her shoulders jumped a little, like a hiccup.

Then she began to knit again, sighing. She knitted as fast as she could, her fingers making scarves and socks and sweaters because they were afraid to be still.

Maxine put her coffee cup on the floor. She glared at Jewell. Fat right she had to go on and on about what Mama had done to *her*. Mama had always given Jewell the best clothes, let her wear make-up, given her money, let her pick the TV shows. And Maxine was never old enough until she left home. Maxine had never been good enough to do or be anything.

If it hadn't been for Jewell, Maxine would have been prettier and better dressed. She wouldn't have had scum like Tony hanging around her and could have had a man with money and a steady job like Clifford only without that fat belly and stupid smile. Clifford could only eat and make money welding pieces of metal together. Jewell had everything she ever wanted because she was so busy knitting and crocheting and making things from coffee cans and milk cartons to want anything anyway.

Jewell was just like Mama. She was mean and selfish, and Maxine could really picture her whipping some pup of a stepson. Together, Mama and Jewell had almost ruined her life.

Maxine laughed because she knew she was grown up and she was just going to walk out and never talk to her bitch of a sister ever again.

'What's so funny?' Jewell said, offended. 'Maxine?'

Maxine laughed and pinched her own thighs until tears came. Jewell stood up and started toward her. Those horrible crawling hands came closer. Maxine screamed and jumped up. She bashed her shoulder on the screen door as she ran out. Across the yard and into her car, she never looked back though she could hear Jewell's voice calling her name.

She drove for a long time, hardly knowing where she was going until she saw the beach and headed for it. She got out and sat on a concrete post, watching the dull grey waves moving forward.

She felt good. She felt sorry about not having any money, but now she was free. And she could start all over again.

/ The Fisherman /

Les cast his rubber minnow out to the deep-looking pool in Town Lake. He bounced his rod tip, making the minnow dart through the water realistically.

Nothing.

Even at 9 a.m., it was getting hot already. One more cast, he told himself, though he always made about five or six more. His vacation was half over, he hadn't done anything that he'd planned to, except a little fishing. He cast far with the breeze, and let the lure sink.

Strike.

No. Just a snag. But it moved a bit. With the heavy line he'd put on to fish at the coast, he had the strength to haul in a huge old sucker. He reeled; the drag buzzed like a kitchen alarm, but whatever he had a hook into barely moved.

He stopped. Whatever it was, it didn't move on its own. He reeled and pulled in slack, then pulled, walking backward, then reeling. For ten minutes he worked, fairly certain that what he had was neither a fish nor a log. He hoped for an old tireful of antique lures.

It wasn't.

It looked like cloth, maybe an old blanket, tangled around something.

'Oh, Jesus fucking H,' Les said quietly.

He saw a little foot, the tarsals sticking out of half-eaten rotted flesh like toes out of a shoe.

He called Ruth Ann from the police station and explained what he'd fished out.

'That's so awful, Les,' she said with a shuddering sound.

'Do they have any idea who she might be?'

'Well, she's only about three or four years old,' he said. He felt numb after the discovery, the walk to a phone. He'd puked when the cop looked, unwrapped the blanket and said, 'Guess the turtles been feeding on her.'

Les explained to his wife that they were checking their files for recent missing children reports. As he talked on the phone, people walked past him in the hallway, either on one side of the law or another. Some looked cheerful; many didn't. Occasionally, two policemen would wander by talking companionably to each other. Even though the building was relatively new, Les thought about how many murderers and embezzlers must have strolled these hallways.

Ruth Ann was still verbally shuddering. Les stared at the floor. How can someone actually kill another human being, he wondered? *Kill.* Just to break their body in some way and run off and not die of grief or remorse over having done it? What would their dreams be like?

'Les?'

'I'll be home pretty soon. I just wanted to wait around to see if they found out who she was.'

'Okay. Do you want me to fix you some supper?'

'No. Not hungry. Maybe some iced tea, I'm thirsty.' He wiped his mouth, the gesture making him feel like an actor in a desert movie. 'Bye, Ruthie,' he said. A man walked by, his dark eyes sliding over Les. Les turned his back and whispered into the phone. 'I love you.'

'Love you, too,' she said. 'Bye.'

He stood for a moment, trying to remember what he should do next. He was confused. Down the fluorescent-lit hallway, the clerk at the desk shook her head when Les asked her if they had any clues yet.

'Nothing fits so far.'

'Isn't that strange? I mean, how can a kid be missing for a month without the parents saying something?'

'Maybe the parents dumped the kid,' the clerk said. As if

realizing that she'd spoken out of line, she shrugged. 'Well, you never know. Maybe one parent thinks the kid is with the other. Something like that. You never know. You hear all kinds of stories.'

Les was amazed that her job had hardened her so that she could imagine a parent doing such a thing. He secretly felt the child must have been the victim of secret international political terrorism or something larger than just murder. She was only three, for God's sake . . .

'Well, I'm going home. Can I call tomorrow and find out what's going on?'

She nodded, giving him a brief, busy smile. 'Good night.'

Les drove home slowly. In his mind, he could still see what was left of the child's face and all that matted dark hair clinging to her skull.

Who were her parents and what were they thinking?

What would I be thinking, if she were mine?

He pulled over to the curb for a moment. A wash of heavy, fluid depression had begun coursing through him. He didn't want to move or speak. Not even to Ruth Ann. He sat and watched people coming out of the drugstore and going by the sidewalk. Les hated the ugly world that he lived in. For the first time in his life, he had a strong urge just to scream, but he swallowed it.

The kid had been a living person once and now she was dead.

Les hadn't seen that many dead people. Once, when he was about fifteen, he'd seen a truck-motorcycle wreck; bodies had been flung to the grassy roadside, splatterings of blood following their trajectory. Strange, but the thing that had bothered him the most wasn't the sight of the bodies because that had seemed so unreal. Les couldn't keep his eyes off the crumpled truck hood. His imagination followed the vision of the motorcyclist into the grill and off the hood.

What had (his) child seen? The cold water closing over her face?

By the time he got home, he was exhausted. Ruth Ann was watching television. She met him at the door and walked slowly beside him, her head hanging down.

He opened the refrigerator door for tea. Ruth Ann had already poured it into a glass with ice cubes and a lemon wedge. 'Thank you,' he said. He sat down at the kitchen table.

'The news should be on in about ten minutes,' she said. She put her hand on his shoulder. 'It was pretty icky, huh?'

He nodded.

'Did someone interview you?'

'No, I told them I didn't want to be on TV.' He sat with his hand on his chin. 'Someone said maybe the kid's parents did it. Can you imagine that?'

'It happens,' Ruth Ann said, and she left the kitchen.

Les breathed slowly in, then slowly out. He drank the rest of his tea and went to bed.

They had decided not to go anywhere on their vacation this year because Les had wanted to do things around the house. Usually they went to a coastal resort in the north or to the mountains where he could fish for trout. Last year, they'd gone to Colorado where Les had taught Ruth Ann to fly fish. She'd had a good time, but he felt like it was his vacation and not hers. Ruth Ann was a teacher and had all summer off most years, so they always seemed to go where he wanted to go, since he only took two weeks.

He could take more. He owned his own camera repair business, so he could take off as much time as he wanted. But Ruth Ann probably wouldn't want to spend his sort of vacation for more than two weeks.

The day after he found the little girl in the river, he mowed the lawn and cleaned up the garage. He found his glove from the time he'd been on a softball team. Ruth Ann was quiet all day. She sewed new curtains and took her car in to get new tires.

At dusk, he found her reading a novel. He plopped down

on the sofa, knowing that because he was watching her she would put her book down and smile at him. 'You look pretty today,' he said after she'd done what he'd anticipated.

After he took his shower, he found her between the sheets. They made love slowly. He held onto her for a long time afterwards, but even her smell and closeness couldn't comfort him. He put his palm on her belly.

He sighed.

'What's the matter?' she asked.

'Maybe we should have had children,' he said.

He heard her draw in breath. When he looked at her face, he saw an angry, wounded expression. The issue had been 'settled' years ago with Ruth Ann's 'Well, if you make me choose between you and having children, of course I choose you.' But even at the time, he knew her reconciliation to his lack of desire was bitter.

Now, it was too late. They were in their forties. The prospect of a child was laced with possibilities of retardation, deformities, other horrors. They could adopt, but the truth was, they had settled into their lives. With hobbies, business and career, childless friends, their schedules were full.

They could rearrange. But it was flatly too late. The time of energy and the will to reproduce and be mummy and daddy was gone.

'Les,' Ruth Ann said. And then she turned her face into the pillow.

He touched her shoulder, then rubbed her back for a long while. It was too late. Too late. And now Ruthie was hurt.

Les felt hollow, the hollowness pushed up in his throat. 'Damn!' he said, and got up and dressed. He wanted to blame Ruth Ann for it all, for pushing him about it years ago. He hadn't been ready and he had only gotten more stubborn as she persisted. He remembered his old feeling about 'messing up their life' with noisy obnoxious brats.

He walked out into the yard and hung his arm over the slender limb of the peach tree that they had planted about five years ago.

He didn't want just *any* kid anyway. He wanted *that* one – the dark-haired 3-year-old that had been cast in the lake. He wanted her back, whole and living, holding her arms up to him.

He grieved for her.

Ruth Ann came out and leaned her cheek on his shoulder. Later they went out to dinner and a movie.

The police couldn't piece together anything about the little girl.

He was glad when he managed to get through the weekend and his vacation and back to work. He could have gone back early, but Ruth Ann wouldn't have understood. He'd done everything he'd planned to around the house – built new bookshelves for the den, fixed the back screen door, repaired the fence where the wind had cracked it, tuned up his car.

Keeping busy had been important.

But even at work, he'd gone on thinking. Haunting him was the decayed face plastered with that still soft and dark hair that he'd seen when the policeman opened up the blanket. He dreamed about her sometimes. In his dreams, a woman chopped the child to bits and alternately threw pieces of her in the lake and fed them to a stray dog. He could only stand and watch, the child's face looking up at him like a moving mask, only inches from the toes of his jogging shoes.

He became a cranky boss to his three employees. His surprised helpers secretly gave each other worried looks and became silent. He tried to make up for it by being extra jolly sometimes, but they shrank from that, too. Eventually, he was quiet and barely spoke as he helped in the shop with the camera repair, or in his office with the books.

As a young man, he'd taken photography courses at a junior college. He'd almost gotten his associate degree and probably could have become a portrait or industrial photographer of some sort.

But that wasn't what he wanted. Winning Pulitzer prizes, capturing the times artistically, fame and greatness. That was what he hungered for.

Through school, he noticed that others were better by instinct. They were artists born, and no matter how he struggled and practiced and studied, he didn't have great talent. Never would he produce the hardcover with slick pages of his photographs to go in oversize bookcases around the world.

So he learned to repair cameras because he loved and respected the machines and he knew he could do that as well as anyone else, perhaps better than most.

It was a great relief to do something 'practical,' as everyone called it. He made a good business of it, even becoming self-employed. And he didn't have to compete and fail.

Sometimes, he felt cheated.

Cheated of what, by whom, he didn't know. But it made him feel closed-up for a long time. He was acquisitive because he was restless. Now he had everything he wanted, including a wife who was a sweetheart, too.

Everything but the little girl he'd fished out of the lake.

Standing in line in the supermarket after work, he held the cold milk against his chest, the bag of peaches and coffee in his hands. Before leaving work, he'd called the police again. 'No clues,' they'd said. He was feeling raw.

Someone was running around town who had killed a child. Les stared at the people in the supermarket. Most stood with accepted boredom, usually staring absently into the next person's groceries. Over there, a man with curly hair. He could have been the one, with that face. Or there, that harridan who looks like she's wrung life out. Or that careless young couple there; some youths are so cold and wild these days.

They all could have done it.

Maybe they've all done something like that, he thought. There are just more of them than fishermen.

They went to the library on Saturday morning. Ruth Ann headed off toward the fiction while Les fiddled with the card catalog. He didn't really know what he wanted. He stared into the microfiche screen without seeing anything that appealed to him.

He decided to check out some photography art books. Lately, he'd started thinking about taking pictures again. He walked toward the quiet carpeted stairway.

He looked up.

A child looked down. She was probably Hispanic, with great brown eyes, and long dark brown hair pinned back at her temples with orange barrettes. Smiling shyly, she twisted and turned on one foot as she clung to the rail.

Les walked up the steps. 'Hi,' he said to her. When she smiled more widely and turned away to hide her face, he put his hand on her head. Then he took it away gently.

He felt confused again, just as he had at the police station. The photography books were on the third floor. He couldn't remember where the elevators were until he saw them. When he got to the third floor, he walked toward the books, but he was suddenly strangled by the quiet and the awesome indifference of the library and the people wandering within it.

He took the fire stairs and ran down the slippery grey steps, his feet echoing through all the floors above and below. He hurried outside and was equally oppressed by the hot, humid sun.

Touching the little girl had filled him with a kind of pain. Never before had he felt such a thing. Lust, affection or distaste had risen in him after contact with other humans, but this time a deep feeling of loneliness and regret lingered stronger than any lust.

I'm going crazy, he thought, and he was afraid. He paced back and forth on the white bricks while cars flowed and idled in the cycles of the traffic lights. He thought of Ruth Ann and how he must not go crazy because she shouldn't have to go through that.

It had been just a kid, just hair and bones. It wasn't mine. No one knows *who* she was. What do I care? And he circled the bicycle rack with his arms crossed over his chest.

Ruth Ann came out with her hands empty.

'Les?' she said, standing with her profile to the sun, squinting one eye at him. 'What's the matter?'

Les wanted to put his arms around her and hold onto her in front of the main library on Guadalupe Street. But he kept his hands crossed, under his armpits. His throat was tight.

'Ruthie, I'm sorry,' he finally said. He was afraid that he was actually going to cry. Break down and cry in front of the whole world.

Ruth Ann tilted her head. She looked as though she were afraid to ask what was on his mind. 'What are you talking about?'

'Our . . . not having children.'

Ruth Ann turned away from him. She looked down the street, south, toward the river. Finally, she turned back to him. 'Bury it, Les. I did and you can, too. Just bury it.'

'But, I . . .'

'I don't want to hear it now,' she said. 'You should have thought about it ten years ago.'

Startled because he'd expected sympathy, Les watched her walk back into the library. Is this how I'd made her feel then, he wondered?

He walked slowly to the car. Sitting on the hood, he waited for Ruth Ann, hoping that she would return to him.

/ Belling Martha /

Martha was looking for her daddy.

By the time she saw the lights of the cabins on the stark hillsides outside the gates of Austin, she'd nearly forgotten her goal. Especially as she knew not to travel by road, it had been enough to survive one hill, the next, and then another . . .

She sniffed the frigid wind blowing toward her from the notorious stove vents of those who lived just outside the city.

Someone was roasting human flesh in their fire.

The thin leather boots issued by the Central Texas Christian Reform Camp were scant protection for slogging through two feet of snow. Breaking the icy crust had made her shins sore, even through her jeans. Wind flapped her sleeves and collar and battered her ears until a dull ache throbbed through her skull. She'd stopped three times on the way from Smithville to build a fire and revive her feet, and sleep a bit.

The aroma quickened her progress. It had been a long time since Martha had smelled that particular odor. The biscuits and apples she'd carried with her – stolen from the camp kitchen – had long ago been eaten.

The closer she struggled toward home and warmth, the more stinging the dry snow felt. Gradually, she could discern details of the cabin she'd spent most of her life in – the heavy drapes at the window, the flat boulder that she used to perch on while she watched her father chop wood, the daub patches on the east wall.

Wise enough not to approach the house from the road, where stray travelers, legal or not, were watched with interest, she came upon the rear door. She pushed it open and stepped inside.

'Daddy?'

The house had changed only a little – different colors and smells; she noticed that her small bed was gone from beside the fireplace. On the stone of the hearth, a cracked head and shoulder lay with its hair stiff and awry. Strips of flesh hung from hooks above the fireplace, and a kettle bubbled on the high grate above the fire. The meat smelled old. It was apparently not a kill, but probably a body tossed out the gates because there was no one to pay for a burial inside the city.

She heard a sound behind her.

'Dad . . .' she said, turning.

A woman was poised toward Martha, holding a garrotting wire in her hands. Martha stepped back and knew as she spoke that she was imitating the cool of her father's manner. 'Hey, neighbor,' she said.

The woman's eyes narrowed. She was still ready to strike. Martha would have to work fast to get out of the situation if the woman was a Crazy.

'Neighbor?' the woman repeated.

'What are you doing in my house?' Martha said.

The woman smiled wryly. 'Like hell *yours*, kid. I live here.'

Now Martha speculated. It had been over a year since her father's last letter had reached her at the camp. Could it be that he'd found himself a companion? 'With my daddy?' she asked.

'Don't think so,' the woman said. Her hands lowered a bit. 'Not unless the old fella hasn't told me all.'

'My daddy's Harry Jim Skill.'

'Well, then, your daddy ain't here,' the woman said irritably. 'What are you doing out here anyway?'

'Looking for my – '

'Yeah, okay,' the woman said. She unwound the wire from her hands and stuffed it into her pocket. 'He didn't teach you a bit of sense, did he? If you're really neighbors with folks like us, I'll let you go. Go on now!'

Martha wasn't ready to have the decision made for her. She couldn't believe her father was not nearby. She shouted, 'Harry Jim!'

'You little fish, I'll stew you . . .' the woman said, walking toward her again.

The back door swung open. Martha swiveled to look. The face could have been handsome or beetle-like, she didn't notice, but it was wrong, all wrong, and that made it horrible.

'Git!' the woman shouted, and Martha hesitated only long enough to shake the uncertainty of terror out of her bones, then pushed through the front door.

As soon as she came in sight of the city gates, she knew she'd lost her caution. She stopped. Before her was the battered sign on a brick wall just outside the gates:

WELCOME TO AUSTIN, TEXAS STATE CAPITAL.

Above her, the sentry leaned out of his watch booth, sighting her down his gun barrel. 'Don't move,' he said through a loudspeaker.

Martha stood completely still. For the first thirteen years of her life – until she'd been taken to the camp – she had seen the walls of Austin, but she'd never been so close as now.

'Drop that bag.'

Martha let her bag of possessions slip from her hand onto the frosty mud.

Still, the guard kept his weapon on her. 'Do you have a pass?'

She started to say no, but thought better of it. 'I got jumped in the back of a government truck. They stole my pass, then shoved me out. Been walking for three days.'

The sentry paused. After a moment, the box that he stood in eased down the wall on a track. When it was about a meter from the ground, it stopped with a mechanical bounce. One of the spotlights atop the wall swiveled until it shone directly on her. She raised her hand to shield her eyes.

'Throw your bag over here.'

Martha picked up her bag and flung it toward the box. The sentry moved cautiously, watching her, and stepped sideways to pick the bag up with a hook. He examined it inside his box. 'Take your clothes off.'

'It's too cold!'

'Do you want inside the city?'

She peeled everything off, including her boots, shivering so hard that she could barely throw the heap toward him. After a few moments, the voice in the loudspeaker said, 'Come in.' The gate opened just a bit; Martha squeezed through the opening. Someone grabbed her arm as she entered. Peripherally, she saw the sentry box rising up the wall again.

She stood naked inside the gates of the city – for the first time. Trampled pathways glittered coldly under the bowed heads of street lamps. Small houses shouldered one another as if for comfort, their windows dark. The wind whined eerily through broken panes of glass. The sound of loose metal clanged in the wind.

She'd imagined cities to be clean havens for good folk but it looked more miserable than outside to her. Still, she thought, surveying all the possible places for residence, there must be a lot of food here . . .

The soldier who held her arm stared hard at her face. 'What's your name?'

Martha blinked. 'Uh . . . Martha . . .'

'Hey, Carrie,' called the sentry above. 'Take my post a while.'

'Shit,' the soldier with Martha muttered. 'Come on down,' she said impatiently. As the other hurried down a metal stairway, she took on a warning tone. 'You're going to get caught one of these days, you horny dog. Someday the governor's daughter will come through WP.'

'This isn't the governor's daughter,' he said, taking

Martha's hand. 'Come on, now, I got to check you in. You want in the city, right? You got relatives?'

As he pushed her toward a metal shed, Martha said, 'Don't know if they're still in the city.' She was getting hazy from the cold and from being shoved around.

'We'll just find out in a little while.' He opened the door. In the shed was a table with tools, greasy notices pinned on a board, and the kind of radio she'd seen in Brother Guy's office at the camp. Against one wall, a cot listed in a mended way.

'Lay down, spread your thighs. Ever done this before?' he asked, unbuckling his coat.

Martha tested the cot and figured it would hold her. 'Do I have to?'

'Sure would make things easier for you, sweetie.'

She shrugged.

The jeep shot through the city, sometimes leaping off crevasses in the streets, sometimes jerking to avoid potholes, sometimes dipping one wheel in a hole with a thump. Martha sat beside the policeman driving, hunched over the bag in her lap.

They'd found her Aunt Jenny Skill in the directory. Martha couldn't remember much about what her father's sister had become, except she'd married in the city and either left or lost her husband. The check-in police told her that if her Aunt Jenny couldn't (or wouldn't) take her in, she would have to go to the WP camp.

Martha knew vaguely about WP camps. Sometimes they kept people doing construction or working in government janitorial jobs for years. One could get out by playing political or buying a bureaucrat's attention. Martha figured her aunt might know where her father was; even if he'd gotten stuck in a camp himself, she could find him. He would help her. Wouldn't he?

She thought about the last time she'd seen him . . .

'Renounce your ways!'

She'd run outside to see the battered truck with a chicken wire cage on the back. Standing inside the cage was an old woman with two apples in one hand and a potato in the other. Though she was grey and fragile, when she spoke to Martha straight through the cage, she had a strong voice.

'Renounce your ways!' she shouted, then pointed to Martha's father standing just behind her. 'Come with us to the Lord's commune. We have food, we have warmth. Don't let your child be damned by your sinning ways!'

'Martha,' her father said, but then was silent.

'Look at all the food,' Martha said, noticing the lumpy bags of potatoes, apples, beans, and cheeses with heavy rinds in boxes, loaves of bread wrapped in paper.

Forty miles to happiness,' the woman shouted. 'Forty miles to regular meals, a warm bed, and God-given peace of mind.' She beckoned to Martha with an apple, unlatching the door of the cage. 'You won't have to eat the flesh of your brothers and sisters. Brothers and sisters in God's eyes! Renounce your ways! We understand! We forgive! We will save you!'

'Martha,' her father said again with a voice as soft as snowfall, 'do you want to go?'

Martha looked at more food than she'd ever seen at once in her life. She thought of the nights that her father wept and sighed after an especially trying capture and kill. She was still young enough to believe that a different life meant a better life, and if her father was willing . . .

'Yes!'

'Come, child,' the woman said, 'come with us to pray with thanks for salvation.'

Martha caught hold of the tailgate of the truck and boosted herself up to the cage door. Then she looked over her shoulder and saw that her father was standing still, just watching.

'Daddy!'

The woman grabbed her shoulders and pulled her headlong into the truck, shouting, 'Take off, Brother Guy!'

The truck lurched. Martha skinned her knees falling forward. She crawled up to look out at the figure standing down the road and screamed, 'Let me out, let me out, you old bitch!'

And far away, her father yelled her name through cupped hands. 'Martha, I love you!'

From the jeep she could see broken-down houses. To her left, she noticed the tall outline of buildings she'd seen distantly for years. They seemed close and large, and yet still a coherent shape.

A wish came to Martha – perhaps if she couldn't find her father, maybe her aunt could take his place.

After she'd first been taken to the Christian camp, she'd been bitter and angry, feeling deserted by the only person that had ever meant anything to her. His few letters to her there had eventually made her realize that he had thought it was the best thing for her. During the numb years at the camp, Martha mouthed the phrases and sang the verses, but they hadn't touched her. She'd make adequate, tentative friendships, but none so profound that she would grieve at separation.

She leaned back and slid down the seat, face turned outward passively to watch the scenery. She'd seen pictures in old books of cities, but all this seemed a ruined imitation. Dried weeds poked out of the thin crust of snow. Parts of houses had been hacked away, probably for firewood or to patch other houses. Fleetingly, she saw someone prying a window frame from an abandoned garage. She saw one tree enclosed within a fence.

Slowing down, the driver spoke for the first time to Martha. 'Is this it?'

Martha looked at the house beyond the posts of what had once been a chain-link fence. The house was a square two-story with symmetrical windows. 'I don't know,' she said.

She followed the policeman up the path to the house. The roof overhung the door a bit, but looked chopped away. A layer of gritty snow covered the boxes and other odd shapes on the porch. The policeman pounded on the door and turned toward the street uneasily.

When the door opened, four people stood behind a heavy mesh. Others looked through the parted drapes. The policeman unfolded a piece of paper and held it out. 'Is there a Jennifer Skill here?'

It reminded Martha of the time she'd first arrived at the camp. Faces, faces, looking back at her.

A woman came forward out of the other room and stood behind the mesh. 'What do you want?'

Martha couldn't superimpose her father's stories of his childhood companion on this tight-lipped, thin woman.

'This girl claims you'll take her in.'

Jenny Skill looked at Martha speculatively. 'Who is she?'

'Martha Gail Skill, she says,' said the policeman.

'Where's my daddy?' Martha asked her.

No answers came for a moment. The policeman and Martha stared inward and the others stared outward and no one said anything. Jenny reached above her head and there were sounds of metal locks slipping as her hands crept down the side of the mesh.

The door opened. Martha stepped inside and stood behind her aunt. The policeman thrust his notebook in the door. 'Sign this,' he said. 'She has no papers. You'll have to get them for her in ten days or pay the fines.'

Jenny only nodded as she signed the paper.

After the policeman left, Jenny took Martha's coat collar between her thumb and forefinger and guided her into the living room. Furniture crowded the room, as if several households' worth of things had to be arranged in a single place.

Fifteen or so people came into the room, some sitting on

the sofas or chairs, but most stood around them. Jenny lifted her chin. 'She's kin to me and I'll take responsibility for her. You know that she's my brother Harry's kid, but she won't pull anything here.' Then Jenny took Martha's jaw in her hand and jerked her face around so that Martha stared straight into Jenny's eyes. 'Will you?' she said.

'Where's my daddy?' Martha whispered. She felt a cramping in her lower gut. The bright electric bulb overhead, the strangers all intent on her presence, and Jenny's roughness confused her.

'Poor thing,' one of the grannies whispered.

'You just forget about your daddy,' Jenny said. 'He's not here.'

'But where is he?'

'No use worrying about it.'

'Now, wait a minute,' a man said.

Jenny let go of Martha and for the first time she was able to focus on the people around her. There were two old grannies sitting together. There were several men about her father's age, and even more women. Younger people nearer her own age numbered only about five. Later, she discovered that six children had been put to bed.

The large man who'd spoken shouldered closer. He had an aggressive, troubled kind of look that Martha had seen on some of the Crazies at the camp. 'I don't feel safe about having your brother's kid here. Nothing against you, Jenny, but we all know what your brother was, and what's to say – '

'Tell 'em where you've been,' Jenny said, nudging Martha.

Martha stood dumbly. She'd heard the word *was* referring to her father. Was? What did it mean?

'She's been in the Christian Reform Camp,' Jenny said. 'Okay, look, Darren, we'll move Terry out of the closet under the stairs and hang that big brass bell over the door. Anyone will hear her coming out at night. Send her out with the kids to scavenge. If she gets fed like the rest of us, she won't be looking to carve anyone up.'

'You'll have to feed her better than that,' one of the grannies said.

'Well, where am *I* going to sleep?' one of the young ones asked. She was kind of pretty, but she kept narrowing her eyes at Martha.

Martha listened vaguely as sleeping places were re-arranged. Someone was sent to lock up the knives in the kitchen. Jenny searched Martha's pockets. Sweat formed on Martha's upper lip; she clenched her teeth as her bowels churned nervously.

'Jenny,' she said, 'what happened to Daddy?'

Jenny turned quickly. 'He's dead! Now I don't want to hear another word about it.'

Martha nodded slowly. She had expected her to say exactly that, but somehow she couldn't believe that she really had. Her ears buzzed and she felt weak. 'I need to go to the john.'

'Kaye, take her out back,' Jenny said.

A young dark-haired woman shuddered melodrama-tically. 'Me?'

'All right, all right,' Jenny replied impatiently. 'Switzer.'

A blond, rosy-cheeked young man motioned to Martha. She followed him through the kitchen, which was clean, but dishes, boxes, cans and bottles were crammed together on narrow shelves and utensils and pots hung everywhere there was room. Switzer unbolted the back door. She saw the john and ran for it.

She stayed longer than she needed to, in spite of the cold, rocking back and forth, sobbing. She thought of the last time she'd seen her father, the words he'd written to her about how they would go south together someday when he had money to pass the boundary. She revived old memories of him telling her stories, the little jokes they had with each other, songs he would sing while cooking or sewing, the way he looked when he was 'just thinking.'

She didn't want to go back inside with those people. At the camp, everyone had done their best to act nice, though the feelings were usually at odds with their behavior.

She stopped crying. She felt dry and cold and used up.

On the way back into the house, Switzer said, 'I'm sorry about your father.' There was a sort of anger in his voice.

Jenny met her in the kitchen and led her to a dim room lined with several mats. Two small forms lay under blankets, but the rest were flat. 'Here. We're giving you a warm place. Keep that in mind.' Jenny opened a closet door. A bell jangled. One of the sleeping children sat up. Martha saw that the dark closet was the inverse shape of a stairway, lined with boxes and tools, all of which seemed to lean dangerously inward. Jenny urged Martha forward.

The door shut behind her with another jangle, then a bolt slipped into place.

She sank down, only then realizing her weariness. As her eyes adjusted to the darkness, she saw the ghost of her hand against a rough blanket. Voices and footsteps scattered randomly around her. Someone went up the stairs above her.

She was hungry – awfully hungry – now. Beyond her door were so many people.

She knew her own ribs and hip bones and spine as hard places on her body. But there were those in the house who were not so lean. She could crawl from mat to mat and search for their hip bones and find none so sharp as her own.

'People are not food,' Brother Guy had said to her on her second day in the camp. 'When God gave Moses the laws, he said 'Thou shalt not kill.' It's better to die of hunger than to kill your fellow man. It is wrong, Martha, *wrong*. You will pay for doing wrong by torment of eternal fire, eternal pain, eternal sorrow in the depths of lonely Hell if you don't get on your knees right this moment and swear – swear! – to God that you were wrong. That you will no longer eat the flesh of humans. That you were an innocent child of circumstances. That you beg His forgiveness. That you repent with a soul full of anguish and remorse. That you will face hunger with a heartful of love for Him! On your knees and pray, Martha! Pray for your soul!'

And Martha had gotten to her knees and prayed, hoping that would relieve all the fear. But over the years, she'd come to recognize that Brother Guy didn't see the world the way she did. In fact, he saw things differently from almost everyone else. Her hope of salvation and fear of an infinite Hell broke little by little, until she behaved the way they expected her to merely out of custom – and respect for the supper table.

Now she was free of that.

When Aunt Jenny fetched her from the closet in the morning, she dragged Martha to a tiny room with a disconnected bathtub. Tepid water still stood from probably two or three others' baths. Martha didn't relish wallowing in scummy water, or that dampness after washing. They hadn't made her wash but once a week at the camp.

'Wash your hair, too,' Jenny said, closing the door.

She obeyed out of habit. Half-way through her bath, someone tossed in a shirt and pair of pants for her, which were slightly large when she dressed. Outside the room, Switzer sat on the floor, apparently waiting for her. 'Hungry?' he asked.

Martha knew that her face changed with the suggestion of food. Switzer led the way back to the kitchen. Six or seven people crowded the room, fixing their breakfasts, washing up, or passing through and chatting.

Switzer motioned for her to sit. Taking the edge of the bench at the table, she noticed the lull in the conversation. A boy stared at her, but the weak-chinned man resumed eating, and the woman stared out of the window. Switzer returned with two bowls of white mealy soup and a chunk of bread. He tore the bread, gave her half, and began to eat rapidly.

As she began to spoon in the cereal, the man glanced toward her with a studied casualness, as if curious about the table manners of her kind.

She didn't waste time on manners.

As she stuffed the last of the bread in her mouth, Switzer said, 'Let's go.'

'Go?'

'C'mon.' He strode across the room. In the entry hall, he put on a coat and knitted cap; his fair hair stuck out around his collar. He wrapped his throat with a cloth sack. Martha found her own coat on a peg.

'Where are we going?' she asked as they walked away from the house. The day was clear but for a few grey clouds in the south, but the sunlight was dulled by a persistent chill breeze.

'Scavenging,' he said. He looked at her sidelong. 'You've gone scavenging, haven't you? Yesterday I brought home a whole door.' He sensed Martha's skepticism and touched the bag around his neck. 'I chopped it up first, of course.' And then he opened his coat and showed her a small axe hanging in the lining of his coat.

They walked without conversation for a long while. All the uninhabited houses she saw had been plundered. Inedible and non-fuel trash hugged chain-link fences. Ahead was the tall yellow tower she'd often seen in the distance.

'This used to be the University,' Switzer said.

They passed into an open area which was crowded with hand-built shacks.

'There used to be trees everywhere,' he continued. 'I've seen pictures of this place where all this was green grass except for walkways, and there were trees . . .'

Martha had seen an area covered with trees outside of Smithville once.

'Maybe it will warm up before we have to ruin every-thing.' Switzer said.

'Warm up?' Martha said. 'Hah.'

'It might.' Switzer slowed down. 'I've read that this is a temporary thing, not an actual climatic change. An aberration because of those three volcanoes and a fluctuation in the sun. If it goes on for another twenty years or so, then it might really be a permanent change, but it *could* warm up.' He was straightforward, not fanatical like the Christians; Martha could see that it meant a lot to him.

But she didn't understand what he was saying. 'Oh,' she said, and squinted.

He smiled vaguely, as if knowing that she didn't follow.

'I don't know any different from now or the good times, anyway,' she said. 'My daddy told me a little about how it used to be, though. It just sounded like stuff he made up. You know how they talk.'

'We'd be happier.'

They were walking through the shacks. Martha saw faces listlessly watching from windows that had once been in automobiles. Even inside the scrap metal and cardboard huts with makeshift stovepipes, the occupants' breath condensed in little puffs. Only a few moved around outside their shanties, hands and feet and heads wrapped in rags, nostrils frosty. Martha thought they looked dulled somehow. She'd seen more people inside the city who looked like they belonged in the Other Yard at the camp than she imagined possible.

Even Switzer was subdued as they quietly walked the edge of the village-within-a-city. He glanced uneasily over his shoulder as two, then three men trailed them as they moved toward the street. Martha flinched when Switzer took her arm, but he held on.

'It's slippery here,' he said, indicating the steps ahead. Martha figured that was an excuse.

When they had descended, Switzer walked at a faster pace. Martha saw that those who'd been following stood like sentries at the edge of what used to be the campus.

'I thought you should know this place,' he said. 'And now you know where *not* to go.'

Martha shrugged. 'What would they do to *me*?'

He didn't answer.

They walked for a long time. Martha's feet began to grow numb and she had chills between her shoulder-blades from the wind. The buildings around them were taller and closer to the street as they moved forward. Fractured glass, abandoned brick and concrete – she realized that was the insides of the city she'd only viewed from afar – not the spun-sugar she used to imagine.

'Pigeons,' Switzer said, pointing to the roof of a three-story building. 'Right in my favorite place, too.' He took a slingshot out of his pocket. Martha wondered how many weapons and tools he carried. They scrounged the ground for chunks of concrete and rocks, or chips of metal.

He let loose with a rock. A burst of pigeons came outward in a wave. He loaded and reloaded with dexterity but out of the ten or so birds only one dropped. They both ran to retrieve it from the middle of the street.

Martha saw that the bird still fluttered and twisted its neck. 'Let me,' she said, holding her hand out for the slingshot.

Switzer handed it over. She looked up at the ridge just below the roof where the pigeons were settling again. The sky was a flat grey now, the clouds having moved in partway over the city, but it was still bright enough to make her squint. Switzer flushed them again, then she shot with the same speed he had, only this time three pigeons dropped.

'Damn lot of birds here,' she said simply, as they walked toward the kill.

'You do all right,' he said with admiration.

'I've had to.' She remembered her father's coaching – 'Right here,' he had said, tapping his temple, 'hard as you can.'

'At the camp?'

'Yeah.' She handed him one of her birds so that they each carried two. 'They took care of us so that we could hunt, farm and chop wood for 'em. They've got one of those greenhouses the government gives out to folks they like.'

'Why did you leave the camp?'

Martha shrugged. 'Just seemed like the right time.'

'Were they mean to you?'

Martha looked at the sky. A bleak day altogether. The only vivid color was the pink weather-pinch in Switzer's cheeks. 'I don't know . . . Naw. They just didn't pay much attention unless you got out of line.'

'Did you?' he asked, smiling conspiratorially.

'Sometimes.'

Martha had been standing in the short-season garden with three others when old Randall fell. He'd had attacks before, but they'd been mild and a few days of resting had usually put him back on his feet.

This time he pitched face forward into the mud, scattering the basket of asparagus he'd gathered at the fence's edge. The four of them watched, and each of them knew the thoughts of the others without so much as an exchange of words or glances.

They waited.

Summer, Martha remembered, and the sky was cloudy without thunderheads, threatening only to blow over without rain. A mockingbird made a sound like a dry wooden wheel squeaking. Martha stood, not even waving away the gnats.

Old Randall made no move.

At first they walked calmly, then more rapidly toward the fallen man. The dry grass shushed under their bare feet as they ran.

No one ever found the bones of old Randall. God moved Brother Guy to leave twenty children without food (only two of whom had the memory of fat sizzling on the fire and a full stomach) just in case they'd forgotten that they lived in His mercy.

They swung their pigeons in tandem as they wandered the city. Switzer talked about things that she couldn't really understand. Like trying to imagine the shape of the city if she'd only seen the ruins they'd passed through, she couldn't follow his words.

'We're driven to excesses,' he said. 'If we have food, we eat it until it's gone. If there's more than we can eat at once, we eat until we're sick, and go back for the rest before we're hungry. If we have enough fuel, we burn it until we're hot, even if the next day we have to be cold again. People are stupid and greedy when they're hungry and cold. If the government hadn't deserted us, they would try to fix things. But everyone with money and power moved to the equator. We've been deserted. After the Tropical War, they took all the people who could help away from the situation, and now they've forgotten.'

'What about the governor?' Martha asked, trying to take part.

'Oh, he's greedy, too,' Switzer said with disgust.

As they crawled through empty structures, overturned heaps of trash, opened cans and boxes and wrecked cars, he talked about scientific farming in cold weather, building places to live in space, and the lack of research in fission, solar power, and other energy sources.

'They were working on all those things before the weather changed. But it was all so half-hearted because they never really believed we would need it. By the time we did, everything was too ruined to make any constructive moves. My parents owned a company that designed solar homes.'

Martha wondered if his parents lived at the house, and what 'solar homes' were, but didn't ask.

He was quiet as they headed back. The kind of quiet that sounded like he was trying to think of something to say. Finally, he asked, 'Can I sleep with you tonight?'

'I guess so,' Martha said. 'But . . .'

'I'll fix the bell. Don't like it anyway.'

The longer she was with him, the more peculiar he seemed, but she thought it would be nice to have someone to play with anyway.

Jenny greeted them at the door when they arrived just after dark. She stared at Switzer a long time, then rifled through their bag and nodded at the pigeons with approval.

'Martha got most of them.'

'Maybe she'll earn her keep then,' Jenny said.

It hadn't been such a good day for the others. For dinner they each ate a few spoonfuls of pigeon and potato in a paste of water, flour, and lard. Martha ate the sparse amount, hoping there would be seconds. There were none. She scarcely spoke a word, but conversation was limited to general comments about the events of the day or the assignment of chores. Martha noticed for the first time that even though her Aunt Jenny said little, most of the conversation was addressed to her, or in her direction, or with an eye for her approval or amusement. It had been exactly the same with Brother Guy at the camp.

Jenny was the head of the house, no doubt.

Martha didn't like her. Simply, without wondering why, she didn't like Jenny's silent appraisal of all that occurred around her. She didn't like the way she held her fork, or tilted her head and half-closed her eyes when someone asked her a direct question. Even the clothes she wore were crisp and characterless. Jenny was neither relaxed nor tense, neither cheerful nor irritable. She was obscure and remote. Martha didn't think of people in intimate enough ways to realize it was this obscurity that bothered her, she only felt that Jenny didn't care for her. In return she didn't like Jenny and that was that.

Switzer was as quiet as herself through the meal. Guessing his anticipation for the night, she smiled a few times.

Jenny gave her choices for evening entertainment: she

could read in one of the upstairs bedrooms until it was time for the children to go to sleep, or play cards in the living room, or just chat in the kitchen and dining room. Martha head mention of a fiddle, but heard no music that evening.

She wanted to play cards when she heard there would be a game. Not since she'd lived with her father had she played. Switzer mumbled something about reading and left the room with a disappointed look on his face.

'Here you go, little Martha,' said one of the grandads, indicating a chair for her. Martha would have felt friendly towards him, but she saw his quick glance at her aunt and felt the politics of the situation. She sat down. One of the other players was Darren, the man who'd spoken against her the night before.

They played rummy for a few rounds without much talk. Martha did all right, but it was obvious that the others played just about every night. She got bored with losing and stood.

'Where are you going?' one woman asked, alarmed. She'd been sitting in a nearby chair the whole time, chatting with the players while she sewed rags together.

Martha just stared at her.

'Where are you going?' the woman repeated in a higher voice.

'I don't know.'

'You just sit back down then,' Darren said.

'Honey, go get Jenny,' the woman said.

They all stared at Martha. Martha stared back. At first, she meant to hold Darren's gaze without flinching, knowing that a straight look was the best way to deal with anger. But something wavered within her and she began to study his throat, his meaty forearm and measured the breadth of his shoulders.

'Jenny!' he shouted. 'Why are you looking at me like that?' he asked Martha, eyes narrowed.

Martha turned away from him. When Jenny came into

the room, each oriented toward her. 'What's going on here?'

'Are you going to let her wander around loose?'

Jenny sighed. 'Come with me.' She took Martha into the dining room and guided her to a straight-backed chair. 'Sit here and just keep away from Patricia and Darren.' And then she was gone again.

Martha watched the children play with jacks and miniature houses built from welded tin cans. They begged attention from adults and older children. The elderly women sat together, as if they could only find interest in each other, occasionally patting a child. The room smelled of damp diapers and old, flaking skin. The women chattered about the people they used to know.

Martha sighed and wiggled in her chair.

'So you're Harry's?' one of the grannies said, noticing Martha's presence.

Martha nodded.

'You look a lot like him, yes,' she said. 'But last time I saw him, he was so changed, you know. It was the first time in . . .' She calculated. ' . . . eighteen years.'

Martha had not dared speak about her daddy. But she found her restlessness disappearing as she leaned toward the granny. 'When did you see him?'

'Oh, it was just last summer. I remember because I was thinking the weather wouldn't be too bad for him at first.'

'Weather?'

'At that prison. In Dakota.' She lowered her voice and peered around the room as if she were about to tell Martha every confidence she'd stored up for several years. 'I think myself that people eatin' people ain't so bad – maybe killin' 'em is. We tried to tell 'em years ago that there were too many people, and that things were going to be bad one way or another. They thought we were just anti-Establishment, you know? Well, we didn't know that the weather – '

'Then he's not dead?'

'Last I heard he was alive. I used to know him a long time

ago. I was a friend of Jenny and Harry's father a long time ago.' The granny smiled.

'Jenny told me he was dead,' Martha said slowly. It was easy for her to believe it had been a lie.

'Oh, I don't think so,' the granny replied helpfully. 'She probably didn't want you running off after him. He talked about you a lot.'

'Sharon,' said the other old woman.

The granny continued in a cheerful way. 'Jenny just knows that you can't go see him. These days family doesn't count for much. It never used to, I thought, but it's even worse now. Why, half the folks that live here don't know if their relatives are dead or alive, and most of 'em probably don't care. Just another mouth, another bed. They'd take a stranger sooner, if he was useful. When I was young, we all believed in love and peace and helping each other . . .'

'Sharon,' said the other again, resting her bony hands on the sagging flesh of her companion's arm. 'These people here, they're like rats. You can't turn your back on any of 'em, and they're still better than some. Remember that.'

'Watch me, Sharon and Candy!' shouted one of the children. 'Watch me!'

Just as the conversation had involved her, it left her again. Martha began to shiver. She turned her head slowly, gazing intently, as if to see through the walls of the house the bell that imprisoned her.

She stirred, hearing a muffled tap at her door. It was an inadvertent sound, followed by more movement brushing against her door. Then the bolt-lock slid.

'It's me.' Switzer's voice.

Martha sat up and drew her knees to her chest. He crawled onto the mattress and pulled the door closed quietly. 'Waring may have heard me. I couldn't tell if he woke up.' He spoke softly and put his fingers on her thigh. 'I brought something.'

She couldn't see him in the darkness, but sensed that he

reached within his shirt. She felt something smooth and hard on her arm. 'What is it?'

'An apple. We can share it. I could only get one this time.'

She took a couple of eager bites and realized that she had eaten her half already. Reluctantly, she passed it over. Her mouth felt rough and dry from its tartness.

'What did you do to the bell?' she asked.

'I tied the clapper with cloth.' He searched for her hand with his. Finding it, he put the apple core in her palm. Martha ate it. He rubbed small circles on her thigh.

She pulled her shirt off over her head, elbows knocking against the boxes around her. 'Hey, Switzer.'

'What?' It sounded as though he were undressing, too.

'Did you know that my daddy was sent to Dakota?'

'Yes.'

'Why didn't you tell me?'

He was silent.

'Is he dead or not?'

'I don't know,' he said. 'The first I heard of that was what Jenny said to you last night. I was going to find out for you. We can't ask Jenny, of course. She knows that you'll try to leave.'

'Why didn't you tell me?' she asked. Her voice rose.

'Shh.' He was quiet for a moment. 'I wanted to wait until I knew for sure, so you wouldn't get your hopes up. And then I thought we could save up some supplies and . . . Well, I want to go with you.'

'With me! To Dakota? Why?'

'Because I want to.'

'Yeah, sure,' she said, 'everybody wants to go to Dakota.'

'You'll see. You remember that I got you an apple? I can do even better than that. We can have everything we need in just a few days, or a week.' He paused. 'I knew you would want to go. I really was going to tell you.'

She believed him. He had an eager sound in his voice. He'd told her before that he'd done a bit of traveling; that would make him a good companion for the road. He gradually moved closer to her and she adjusted with his moves until they were parallel shapes on the shallow mattress.

She could figure the route to Dakota; she'd heard talk about it all her life. It was wretched, even though spring was coming on. Glassy snow covered even the most traveled areas. Open stretches of land made it difficult to travel without goods to exchange for safe passage from those who made their living off highway traffic.

I will need food, she thought, feeling Switzer's skin touch hers. He was warm.

She saw him by her side as they trudged through the snow, talking of times when technology would take care of misery, and everyone would have food and shelter. He was serene and calm, looking forward to things she couldn't see. And vulnerable because she had him in the white light of snow and sun at a casual moment. She drew out of her coat the axe he had lent her.

She dug her fingertips into his shoulders. He was not lean. Everywhere he touched her, she blazed. Never before had she been so warm that sweat was like a mist hovering over her pores. Their breathing, kisses and suppressed voices became a secret between them.

She sliced his carotid easily with the axe and hardened herself against the look of betrayal that became his death mask. Her fingers clamped the wound as he fell, so that the blood flowed into the tissues rather than spilling wastefully on the ground.

Never before had her body been so confusing to her. A feeling overcame her that would have been soothing had it not been so urgent, had it not been pushing her to something further . . .

When the pulsing stopped completely, she dragged him by his coat collar off the road under a clump of shrubs where she quickly gathered stones and built a fire. She heated the axe in the flames until it sizzled when tested in the snow. With one stroke, it would cauterize the flesh it hacked through. First – the

arms, cut through until she could disengage the ball and socket.
Then, the knee joints, then the thigh from the hip . . .

Her breathing spurted from her uncontrolled. Switzer
made a sound that was like weeping, but she felt his face
against hers and it was dry.

'Martha,' he said softly. He didn't speak to reproach her,
to call her attention, or to order her. She hadn't heard her
name said that way for a long, long time, and only by one
other person.

As she dozed, she thought of her father.

She woke, but with the feeling that she'd been coming
awake for a long time.

The night was not hers; it belonged to the people whose
sleeping presences oppressed her. Something obliged her to
remain in the position dreams had shaped for her until the
sound of someone muttering in their sleep freed her from
the silence.

With stealth natural to her, she disentangled Switzer's
fingers from her hair, dressed, and carefully opened the
door.

The bell made a muffled clunk.

She stood for a moment, listening. No one moved. She
made her way to the front hall and found Switzer's coat. In
the pocket, the sling; in the lining, the axe.

She was hungry. She held the axe and stood in the
darkness.

'People are stupid and greedy when they're hungry,'
Switzer had said earlier. She thought of the way he'd said
her name, and she knew what hunger would drive her to.
He was something warm in her life, but she would not
consume it to extinction.

Quietly, she unlatched the door and left, wearing his
coat.

/ Greek /

Most of the voices she heard murmured devotion.

One woman spoke a string of unhesitating syllables, flowing, without emphasis or inflection, a monotone chant. 'Weto pata shan tan pata pata.'

Then, a change. Another voice.

'Ay, kai apo stomakous arnohn tamay nelai kalko kai tous . . .'

Others hushed to whispers, listening. The words were strange and difficult, but lyrical. Not praying. Revealing.

' . . . men katotheken epi kthonos aspairontos . . .'

There were meanings behind the words – pauses, rising and falling of pitch, but the story was buried by the hallelujahs of the Pentacostal Church.

Hannah turned the cassette player off. She dug through the papers and envelopes that cluttered her desk. 'Uhm,' she said, placing the tips of her fingers on her brow. 'I took the tape and your term paper to Dr Van Pelt in the linguistics department. He told me it was Greek, but he hasn't translated it yet.' Apologetically, she looked at her student, who sat silently in the chair across from her. 'I hated to tell him to hurry on it, you know?'

'Greek?' Candy said.

Hannah nodded. 'Van Pelt said – after hearing this – that the man probably knows the language fluently. Do you know anything about him?'

Candy considered. 'Well, the preacher and everyone seemed pretty quiet whenever he started up, like he was really saying something. When the preacher interpreted it, though, it was the same kind of thing he said for the other speakers. You know, God is watching and caring for us. Stuff like that.'

'What did the man do?'

Candy frowned. 'Nothing. I mean, he just seemed like an old greaseball.'

Hannah watched Candy's face for a moment, hoping to see a spark of curiosity or connection. Candy looked at Hannah, waiting.

'Have you ever heard of xenoglossia?' Hannah asked, knowing well that two of the books Candy had supposedly read for her term paper had mentioned it, although briefly. In fact, the subject of glossolalia had to include the debate over whether the languages used were real or not. But Candy's term paper hadn't been much more than a definition of glossolalia and an explanation of her visit with a friend to the church.

'Xenoglossia,' Candy repeated. 'I think I saw it somewhere, but I don't remember . . .'

Hannah waited for Candy to do a little brain-wracking. She suppressed her whole stock of impatient feelings about students who no longer seemed to stretch their minds. They wanted everything told to them simply, then perhaps they would retain it. 'What,' Hannah said emphatically, 'is an old man doing speaking ancient Greek in a Pentacostal Church?'

Candy looked startled, trapped. 'I don't know.'

Hannah smiled. In her teacher's voice, she said, 'I want you to think hard about how this could happen, perhaps in terms of environmental influences, unconscious influences, subliminal learning. Try to find out more about this man from your tape. Maybe he had Greek relatives. Perhaps he knew some Greeks as a child and soaked up the language. But why should he use it like that?'

Candy didn't seem to be paying attention. Hannah felt that she might just as well tell her student that crossword puzzles were the key to all knowledge. 'You want me to go back?' she asked, a small sound of reluctance in her words.

'Well,' Hannah said, 'I thought you might want to check it out. I thought you were *interested* in people speaking in tongues. But I just thought you should know about the Greek, should you decide someday to borrow the work you've done on this paper for another term paper in the future.'

'Thank you, Dr Karel.' Candy gathered her books in her arms, somehow not catching the long silk of her hair in them.

Hannah followed her to the door of her office, like a hostess, while Candy exited. 'See you in class.'

She read through another term paper, sitting on the bed, an afghan thrown over her shoulders, a cup of coffee on the nightstand. She sighed.

'What's the matter?' Ted asked.

'Nothing, really.'

'You seem a little depressed.'

She put her pen down and stared at the paper. 'I'm too idealistic.'

'Ah, burn-out,' he said, sympathetically. 'And so young.'

She laughed. 'No, if I were burned out, I wouldn't feel this sad. It just seems that they don't have much *umph*. I was so full of fire when I was an undergraduate. They don't even seem curious. They have no ideals, no heroes, no great aspirations . . . other than to make money . . . or to have a good time.'

'You're still full of fire,' he said, putting his hand on her knee.

'I thought the student who wrote the paper on glossolalia would be fascinated with the man speaking Greek, but it meant nothing to her. I suspected that any moment she would ask me if I was going to give her a lower grade because he didn't speak like the others, and therefore was a mistake.'

'It's probably always been like that, you just don't remember.'

She looked at him, wanting to believe that it was true. He seemed to be able to stack up facts in orderly rows and give a convincing argument to any issue. But sometimes she mistrusted that, searching for bridges that no one else had yet seen. Could it really be that modern minds were deteriorating?

She shrugged. 'Maybe,' she said.

She paced in front of her classroom. 'I just read an interesting article in the new *Journal of Sociology*. I want you to think about this. There seems to be a decline of old, derelict poor living in the downtown areas of five major American cities. The facts were gathered in a similar way ten years ago and again last year by the same re-searcher. He has presented his data thus.' She drew a grid on the blackboard and filled in numbers, dates, and cities.

She turned to her students. Some seemed alert, some not. 'I know that, to do a proper assessment, you should read the article itself, and read other articles on the same subject. But, pretend that you know a lot about it, and pretend that these facts are reliable, which they might be. Consider: is it possible that these are statistical facts and not real facts? If it is a reality, how has this trend come about?'

Silence. No eye contact.

Prodding them, she asked, 'What happened when these old people were young?'

'Maybe they're just dying off,' one of her more aggressive students said.

'Yes, maybe so.' She calculated. 'They would have been in their prime during the Depression. Do you think that would have been a significant event to this population?'

No one disputed the idea. Most wrote it down in their notebooks.

Another student raised her hand. 'What about social programs?'

'What do you think?' Hannah asked her class. 'Do you

mean social programs for those on the streets or for people before they get to this stage?'

'Maybe before,' the girl murmured, unsure.

By the end of class time, they had discussed governmental budget cuts in social programs, the plight of the old and economically useless in an aggressively money-making society, changes in the family's role and self-expectations. Hannah had dragged every last observation out of them. She heard cynicism. They blandly discussed everything going down the drain, but not in the same way that Hannah felt it.

'Listen,' she finally said. 'It's nearly impossible to do something that you think will be effective in making social changes. But if we all give up and don't even *look*, then what? It is hopeless if no one cares. So, you,' she tried not to, but did point at an especially flip student, 'or you, have to think, you have to know. Situations don't go away if you don't believe in them. And without recognition, nothing of value will ever be done.'

Candy stopped by after class the same day that Dr Van Pelt brought by the translation.

'I haven't had a chance to talk to that old man, you know,' she said.

Hannah was surprised that Candy had even considered it. 'Have you thought about it?' she asked. 'What do you think?'

I don't know,' Candy said, 'I think he's a loon.'

'That's not an answer. Dr Van Pelt said that the man is reciting the *Iliad* almost verbatim.' Hannah watched her student. 'By Homer,' she added.

'That's weird,' Candy said.

'What church is it?' Hannah got out a pen and found a clear space on a file folder to write down the address. Candy paused, as if she realized that she was handing something over that was important, but couldn't manage the strain of carrying it. She gave the address and added a few landmarks. 'I may drop by and talk to him myself,' Hannah said.

'You can't just go and barge in on him,' Ted said to her at dinner.

'I'm not going to – I'm just going to find him after church and talk to him.'

'How are you going to find him?'

'I'll know. He sounds different from the rest of them.'

'What do you think you're going to find out, anyway?'

She shrugged. 'I don't know. My Finnish grandmother used to tell me I would get into trouble all my life because I can't keep my nose out of other people's business. That's why I became a sociologist.' She looked at him seriously. 'Aren't you curious, either?'

He broke another roll from the basket. 'I don't think it's going to be as exciting as *you* think. Besides, I agree with your Finnish grandmother.

The church was not full but it brimmed with spirit. Hannah arrived late and hesitantly broke through that fullness into an empty space on a metal folding chair. The fluorescent light from ceiling panels shone harshly in the square room.

She felt out of place. Even though she had tucked her curly brown hair into a bun and wore her most ordinary – almost housewifely – clothes, her posture, expressions and gestures marked her just as if she'd come in her academic robes.

The people around her sang and swayed, clapping in time. Some of the voices wailed, some were sweet, others only sincere. The preacher called out between clap-beats, 'Love the Lord!' Bewildered babies cried. Hannah sat stiffly, staring at the women's rounded shoulders and the men's shiny hair.

She clutched her canvas bag, feeling like a spy because of the small tape recorder hidden within. She fumbled with a hymnal, suspecting that she could hide her confusion by finding their song. All the while, she felt like a child again. The more enthusiastic they became, the more embarrassed Hannah grew. Like being caught with a book that is trashy, or in clothes that are out of style, but not defiantly so.

Maybe he's not even here, she thought. And it occurred to her that this could mean a lot of discomfort for little reason. Maybe Ted is right . . .

Every now and then a glance from someone reminded her that they knew she didn't belong. These fifty or sixty people probably knew each other well. She imagined them all turning at once to look at her. Silly, she thought, these people are just worshipping God in their way. But she started to gather her things to go.

Then a sudden quiet bade her be still.

The preacher began to talk. His voice was pleading as he told of a man whose daughter had fallen dead only days after he'd denied God. Women wept as the preacher moved to and fro, retelling the anguish of the father. Men bowed their heads and worked their jaws.

Hannah was transfixed. She forgot herself and wondered at the effectiveness of his oration. Like a tidal force, he pulled his congregation back and forth with upturned palms full of accusing words. He pushed his prayer upon them, and drew prayers out as they began to murmur. Hannah could smell the heat rising out of their perfumed deodorants and aftershave.

Someone moaned with a wide-opened mouth, stood, stumbled forward, then collapsed.

Hannah rose in her seat but kept herself from going forward to see. The man on the floor trembled and thrashed his head back and forth as he poured out single and double syllables. 'Blagga tagga do wink,' he said.

The preacher counterpointed. Someone begged for mercy. Another begged Jesus to come into her heart and life. Others came staggering forward, pleading in sounds that she couldn't understand at all. Hannah felt oppressed by the God that they brought down through the ceiling and up through the dusty linoleum.

'Hay ra kai egkos afeken, hekon d'emartanay fotos,' he said.

Hannah jammed her fingers down on 'play' and 'record.'

'. . . pama shatama matama katoo shatami . . . ' another said.

No, no, where did he go? She stretched to look.

And them she saw him – wizened, looking like a reformed alcoholic in his lean raggedness. He stood, eyes closed, gesturing his story.

Following him home, she was not subtle as she rolled and parked, rolled and parked, every block, but her subject was unsuspicious and didn't seem to notice.

She watched him enter an old apartment building. Inside the dirty tiled foyer, she pondered before sixteen mailboxes. Eliminating the couples, the females, she was left with nine featureless names.

The first choice was wrong. She was still dazed from the intensity of the church and expected the young man at the door she'd knocked on to conjure or chant at her. He leered instead.

'Uh, I'm looking for a friend of mine. From church. An older man.'

'Oh,' the young man said sourly, 'you must mean number eight.'

'Thank – ' she said to the closing door.

She hurried down the hall. Through the lacquered door, she heard his voice singing. Before she knocked, she flipped her tape cassette and turned the recorder on, then put it back in her purse.

The subject opened the door to her and Hannah suddenly turned timid as she faced the man standing in his home.

'Hi,' she said, 'my name is Hannah Karel.'

'Hullo?' His eyes were curious and thorough.

'I just came from the church. May I come in and talk to

you?' She sounded unconvincing even to herself. 'I want to talk about . . . speaking in tongues.'

'Yes, Lord love you, come in.'

It didn't fit. Hannah was disconcerted by his manner – a gentle-voiced alkie. But it wasn't fair to judge by his appearance. The room was strange, too. Sketches and paintings of soldiers with spears and arrows, landscapes of rocky shores hung on the walls, most pinned with tacks. Ketchup, salt and pepper had to share the small table with pencils, acrylics and rags. A straight-backed chair stood by the window, which without a curtain allowed flat light to brighten the room. The furniture was broken and mean, but the artwork gave it a garret feel.

'Did you do all these?' she asked, seeing another portrait. Though his hand was naive, Hannah saw power.

'Yeah. I just took up painting a few years ago. Would you like some orange soda?'

'Yes. Thank you.'

'Did you see my exhibition at the church last month?'

'Oh, no, I missed that,' Hannah said uncomfortably.

He had disappeared into another room, which Hannah suspected was the kitchen. Water rushed; she heard metal clink against glass, and a gurgle of liquid.

'How long did you say you've been painting?' she asked. 'You seem a natural. I'm surprised you've learned this much in a couple of years.'

He came back into the room and handed her a glass, then sat in the chair by the window. Hannah wished she had brought her camera – she could see a black and white portrait with harsh light on half his face, all pits, furrows and oil, defined by the merging of sun and shadow, then the night side of greys. She liked the sound of his voice, his big clumsy-looking hands.

'I was a drinker, you see,' he said. 'I thought of nothin' but the bottle and how to get more when I was dry. How to get more when I had enough. And one night, God came to me. He told me – this is true and I'm not afraid to say it –

He told me that He was going to give me spirit because I was empty. And I began to speak . . .' He closed his eyes.

'Speak in Greek.'

'Greek?' he said.

Hannah watched him.

' . . . the words that God gave me to worship Him. And He gave me dreams to go with the sounds.'

'But where did you learn Greek?' she asked.

'I don't know Greek. I don't know what you mean.' He sipped at his soda. 'I love God and I love my dreams. That's why I began to paint. I had to . . . to *do* something. Something to show what I see.'

Hannah looked around at the paintings and sketches. She looked at the portrait of a woman, whose ringlets were dark on her forehead. The stark landscapes, the costumes he dressed his subjects in.

'What does "aspairontos" mean?' Hannah asked.

'What?' He leaned forward and wrinkled his nose.

'"Aspairontos."'

Again, he leaned forward, but this time his hands fell between his spread knees as if he'd just dropped something unimportant. 'The words don't mean nothin', miss, between you and me, except they are the words that come to me. I see things when I say them. But they're just sounds.'

Hannah nodded. She didn't doubt his belief. 'Did you know that you're speaking ancient Greek?'

He stared at her. 'You're not really from the church at all, are you? I thought you'd come to talk about the Lord and pray with me.'

'I'm a sociology professor. I was curious about where you learned Greek and why you recite it in the church as if you are speaking in tongues.'

He looked away from her into the flat light out the window and was still. 'No one else would listen and I have to say the words to see the story. Everyone else just thought I was crazy.'

'The story?'
'The story in my mind.'
But he would say no more about it.

Hannah sat in the kitchen with Dr Van Pelt, his wife and their 18-month-old, who clung to his mother's fingers as he sat on her knee.

'Well, it's definitely Homer, too,' Van Pelt said, moving one piece of paper over another and back again. Sometimes he lifted a paper and peeked under it as if it were a young woman's skirt. 'But not all of it. This isn't in place, at least, and I don't remember it in the work.' He read: '"The mind of man is dying, even their dreams have no new substance."'

Hannah sighed. 'Trouble is, I really believe that he doesn't know what he's saying. Maybe his Jungian archetypes are coming forward.'

'Come on, Dr Karel,' Van Pelt said. He gave her the look probably reserved for students who beg off exams. 'You don't believe that, do you? Even with the human linguistic apparatus being an inherent part of our neurological structure, one must learn the ingredients – the vocabulary – at the very least.'

Hannah shrugged. 'I don't know. Maybe it *is* God.'

Van Pelt and his wife exchanged glances. The baby said something like 'lay-chay' and reached for his bottle. 'I doubt that.'

'I was kidding,' Hannah replied defensively. 'But imagine if Homer was a prophet, then what's the difference between the *Iliad* and the Bible . . . ?'

'It's obvious that you lack theological background, Dr Karel,' he said.

He was not a man who could see another side even for the sake of argument. Hannah had gotten so used to egging her students on to brainstorm a question that she'd forgotten the wall that learning could build around an academic individual. 'Well, what about random duplication of sound?' she asked. 'Just coincidentally, your interpretation of his sound matches closely . . . '

She stopped speaking as Van Pelt shook his head. He pointed to the pages of syllables garnished with dots, double dots, upside-down e's, and vowels jammed together.

'I have trained for years,' he said, looking at her indulgently. He shook his head. 'He's just lying.'

Hannah stared at the papers.

Why did she believe the old man more than Van Pelt and his years of education and research? Not that she disbelieved Van Pelt, either, but something was missing. Obviously, the professor was right about the language.

Obviously.

'Thank you so much for your time, Dr Van Pelt. I really do appreciate it. I'm sure it's cryptomnesia. As soon as I find his learning source, I'll let you know.'

Van Pelt smiled. His wife smiled, too. The baby babbled. 'I would be interested,' Van Pelt said. 'Keep in touch.'

Candy didn't step into her office. She stood in the doorway, her eyes restlessly glancing back in both directions of the hallway.

'I went to his hometown,' Hannah said, rising to meet her student, since the student wouldn't come to her. 'I traced his entire life history, talked to his psychologist at the veteran's hospital. I met his sister. I even went back and talked to the minister at that church, which was a difficult interview to say the least. Nothing. No Greek neighbors, no leads that anyone can give. He never did it until a few years ago. Nothing.'

Candy nodded.

'What do you think?' Hannah asked her.

'Gee, I don't know.'

Candy looked exhausted. She was probably trying to do too much. Remembering her own undergraduate days of classes, boyfriends and part-time jobs, Hannah felt a sudden sympathy. 'Come on in, Candy,' Hannah said. 'Let's try to think of another approach.'

Candy hesitated. 'Well, I really gotta go, Dr Karel. I have to study.'

Hannah moved toward her. 'Are you all right?' she asked.

Candy was mute for a moment, then looked at Hannah with sad, sad eyes. 'I've been having these really weird dreams lately.' Her chin fluttered. 'They're so *real*. They're like a movie.' She hesitated, then burst into tears. 'My mother thinks I'm crazy!'

Hannah shut her office door and listened to Candy's dream of living on steep mountains, spinning raw wool that coated her hands with lanolin, and waiting for the peacock-colorful warriors to come home again. Her mother told her that she *must* be dreaming; Candy felt she was awake and living it.

But her mother would only put her hands over her ears and weep in alarm when Candy talked all that gibberish.

She had always been comfortable on these streets where people lived out of garbage cans, used the sidewalks for their beds and urinals, laid their heads on bundles of newspapers at night.

As a child, she felt 'missions.' Her mother caught her carrying canned goods and blankets out into the suburban streets at night, believing that the poor children that Dickens had written about huddled in doorways. In college, she served up turkey and stuffing to the homeless on holidays before going home to her own family. Even now, she sometimes resented the researching, the preparation for classes, all the things peripheral to the purpose of her life.

And the old men who leered without shame, she pardoned – not excused – and remained tolerant of the grimy old women, carrying their load of tattered shopping bags from the best uptown department stores. Through the years of studying social problems, structures and conditions that led to the rise, fall or stasis in the lives around her, she had hoped never to let people elude her.

She came around a corner in the chilly dawn, and saw an old woman across the street wearing several layers of clothing. The woman stood near the corrugated trash barrel, separating strips of greasy paper bags and cloth into piles.

The old woman muttered.

No. Not muttered. Sang. In a raspy old voice without any rhythm, she sang a phrase, paused with effort in her work, then sang again.

Hannah stood beside her and listened.

She knew the words, knew the tale that the old woman sang. As sure as any memory of her childhood, she remembered her Finnish grandmother reading the *Kalevala*.

'Siina kukkous, kakonen, hekyttele, hietarinta, hiloa hoperinta, tinarinta, riukuttele!'

Hannah recalled the people of her grandmother's tales – Ukko swinging his hammer, wearing a skirt of fire and blue stockings. Aarni, guarding hidden treasures. Good deeds and bad done by colorful people who lived in a ripe land . . .

> Mastered by desire impulsive
> By a night's inward urging
> I am ready now for singing.
> Ready to begin chanting
> Of our nation's ancient folk-song
> Handed down from bygone ages . . .

She looked around. The sun was a blazing red on the edge of a cobalt sky. Birds sang on blossoming trees. Down the street, a man played a flute. Others listened, their faces alive, alert, curious.

Hannah saw a man peer at his companions longingly from a dingy doorway. She turned back to the aged woman poking through the trash. 'Do you speak Finnish?' she asked in Finnish.

'Wha'?' the old woman said.

Van Pelt shook his head. 'Someone once found a fountain pen embedded in sedimentary rock side by side with fossils from the Pre-Cambrian. One could speculate that Martians dropped it during a tour in one million B.C. But there was an explanation.'

Hannah listened to his weary voice. He looked tired and empty to her. 'Yes,' she said gently. 'But that doesn't mean nothing happened. An explanation doesn't wipe out the event. And first someone has to see it to want to explain it. Some things take a different kind of perception than just looking at what's in a rock.'

'I don't understand what you're getting at.'

'I'm sorry you don't,' she said. As she looked at him, she had an uncanny feeling that, where he'd tried to sweep out the enchantment and curiosity in his brain, there now seeped slowly something old but magical.

/ Petit Mal /

It sounded like a door slamming inside my head.

I was tired from working overtime in the chair factory the first time I noticed that anything was wrong. My sister Beth put away the dishes from the drainer while I drank a glass of iced tea at the kitchen table. She picked up a cup and opened the cupboard.

I heard a 'slam' but didn't really *hear* it; I kind of felt it.

And suddenly Beth was kneeling with a saucepan, stacking it into the other pots with a dull clank. – slam – 'I' – slam – 'when' – slam – 'over,' she said to me.

Her movements were jerky. I put my head on my arms. The linen tablecloth was cool. I was tired, but I didn't know that my life was being snatched from me, bit by bit.

I'm in The Place, as we used to call it. The people here seem just to call it In Here. I can't hear them much and I have given up trying to talk to them.

During that first night I felt like I had been trying to sleep for two nights. Every few minutes, I'd come up out of sleep and look at the aqua green dial of my clock as it jumped. I shook the clock. Every now and then it ticked, but it ran about double-speed in jerks.

That slamming was still in my head.

When I slept again, I fell into groaning mouths for what seemed like for ever and couldn't wake myself up again. But when I was awake again, the clock had only ticked off five, seven or ten minutes and then slam! it was a different time again.

I put the clock under the bed and got through the night somehow.

When morning finally came, I heard my mother open my bedroom door and put her hand on my shoulder. 'Fred?' she said. Slam. I rose up when she touched me, but she was gone.

I went down for breakfast. My mother said, 'Hurry!' I ate; my oatmeal was cold before I finished. Mother felt my forehead like she used to when I was a kid. Could she hear the sounds in my head? I felt guilty because I'd taken some fun pills with Joe after work the day before. Maybe this was a hangover. I didn't want to tell her about it.

Beth was there, then she was at the door, leaving.

'Bye,' I said.

I stood on the driveway and watched down the road for Joe to pick me up. It was late summer and the piny woods smelled good and it was cool. I didn't have my jacket but Joe would have his pickup all warmed up with his jokes and his thermos-cup of coffee that he always drank when we rode to work. I scuffed at the gravel and looked up. Joe's pickup was down by the bridge near the Johnson's place.

Slam.

Then it jumped to the McCready's mailbox.

Slam.

Next it was in front of me.

That was the first time I was really scared. Joe opened the door for me. First he smiled, then he looked impatient.

'Something's wrong with me,' I said.

And I had the feeling that this had all happened before, too. I looked at Joe and remembered everything as it happened, but I couldn't remember what would happen next. I felt really cold. Joe moved the truck onto the driveway.

The sun was blinking higher in the sky. Cars and trucks jumped up and down the road. Joe said, 'In,' and he took me back to Mother.

The trip to the Medical Center in the city only took as long as the drive to the county seat. I'd never seen Beth drive so fast, and Mother never said anything to her about it.

We sat in a waiting room, then we were behind a curtain in a big room with lots of beds. Doctors looked at me, touched me, tapped me, made me walk and roll my eyes. I started to tell them about the slamming in my head but every time I began there would be another slam; my mouth would be open and they'd all be turned away from me.

They gave me pills and the glass of water disappeared out of my hand.

No one said much to me. I got in a word or two, but none of it made much sense. I never really knew what anyone was saying, or what they were doing. They took me somewhere on a stretcher. The elevator door closed halfway and opened again, but it was not where we'd started from.

I had a tiny television by my hospital bed, but I couldn't watch it. It flickered and changed and made my head hurt.

The sun went down early in the afternoon, like the world was going crazy. I didn't have time to eat dinner. I could see the hallway from my bed after dark. Most of the time when I woke up during the night the hall was empty, although sometimes people stood and looked at me from the narrow slice of light.

When the sun came up, they brought my breakfast, but I closed my eyes for a minute and it was gone. The maid mopped the floor. She talked to me. When I answered, she was by the bathroom with her back to me. They brought me another breakfast; it was a hamburger. I was hungry, but they took it away again before I finished. It was cold anyway.

Beth and Mother appeared, Beth sitting on the bed and holding my hand just like she used to when we'd do something scary together. She snapped her head back and forth as people jumped in and out of the room, but we didn't talk to each other. And still, I had the feeling that I remembered it all.

The doctors came in for a few seconds. Beth was gone. Mother was in the hall, then she was gone. I wanted to squeeze my head, squeeze the trouble right out of it, but it wouldn't go away.

They brought me an early lunch, or a snack, and I finally got to eat it.

The sun went down at lunchtime. I lay in the dark, dreaming that I was in the hospital, dreaming. The nurse gave me a shot and I slept for two days.

They took me into the elevator again, but this time I never saw the door open or close, I was just in the other room suddenly. They pasted things to my head and took them off.

I was in my room. They brought me breakfast – beef stew and salad. I ate it. Vomit appeared on my bed and my mouth tasted terrible and bitter.

Beth came and sat on the clean bed. Mother sat in the chair.

A doctor came. He'd been there before. He wrote down a note for me. 'We are trying to stop your seizures,' it read.

So I finally understood. I was having fits. 'Little seizures,' the doctor called them, 'without loss of muscular control.' And I wrote to him about how familiar everything was. He said it was 'déjà vu,' because my brain was short-circuited.

I read his note, wrote an answer, and read his explanation between lunch and sundown.

I never went back to work at the chair factory. After I got out of the hospital, Beth took me there to see the gang. The staple guns were going faster than I could see, and some not at all. I couldn't understand anything my friends said as they jumped around me. They stopped talking and went back to work. Joe shook my hand. He looked embarrassed, and then he was gone.

I started reading because books and magazines would keep still for me. Sometimes pages turned over, but I finally put a board across the top of the pages to hold them. I couldn't always concentrate though. It was noisy in my head. Occasionally I saw stars – actually they were more like sparks.

Mother and Beth were always there, but I didn't try to talk any more. I felt dull from the medicine they gave me. Having people around made me jumpy. Especially if they talked. Hearing half a word or the end of a sentence was worse than hearing nothing at all.

I smashed my clock one night because I was sick of time. I was sick of waking up all night long. I was sick of it all.

Everything became like snapshots. Mother outside at the edge of the garden with a basket to pick tomatoes. Beth sitting on the sofa putting on her boots. Slam. Beth standing at the door. Slam. No Beth.

I never saw birds any more. By the time I noticed them, they were flying away.

Mother and Beth started looking older. Sometimes a man came to visit Beth. I think he was a teacher from the town our cousins lived in. Beth brought him to me once; he reached out to shake my hand, then he was in the hallway. I smelled Beth's perfume.

My clothes got too big.

Beth was gone. I didn't see her for a long, long time. Mother brought me pictures of her wedding and I tried to cry but I was dry. I wrote Mother a note, 'Why couldn't I go to Beth's wedding?'

Mother cried. She looked really old.

Every day seemed like half when I first got sick, then it was like six hours, then four. Winter, spring, summer, and fall – weeks to me.

Some days I'm worse. I used to watch the sun jolting across the sky until I thought I may have burned my eyes a little. I was tired. Too tired to move any more. It was hard to explain to Mother that there wasn't much use in getting up and looking after myself. That's when Mother couldn't take care of me any more and I got put in The Place.

I lay on my bed and listened to my body tick, tick between the slamming sounds in my head. I stopped being lonely, but sometimes I still felt like screaming. Even a scream would take all day, and I couldn't waste the time.

Beth came to visit me now and then. I felt her hands getting knobbier and more gnarled each time.

One day I saw a bird. I saw it floating down from a tree, a drop of rain quivering on its wing. The feathers separated as it stretched and tucked its wings back. Strutting, it slowly dipped and pecked at the ground. A pebble ricocheted off and bounced. Dust flew under the bird, shimmering in the sun.

'You're getting better,' the doctor said.

Now I sit and watch the graceful motions of the others In Here. We open our mouths and laughter cascades out as old toothless Louie does his dance. I stand in the cafeteria and watch the plain girl with the auburn bangs in her hairnet ladle out the soup and lift her chin slowly to look at me as I take my plastic bowl.

Sometimes I watch the wind moving in the trees because I think I may be the only person in the world who understands the seconds as they slowly, graciously tick away.

I wonder how long before my sister Beth will visit again.

/ Her Furry Face /

Douglas was embarrassed when he saw Annie and Vernon mating.

He'd seen hours of sex between orangutans, but this time was different. He'd never seen *Annie* doing it. He stood in the shade of the pecan tree for a moment, iced tea glasses sweating in his hand, shocked, then he backed around the corner of the brick building. He was confused. The cicadas seemed louder than usual, the sun hotter, and the squeals of pleasure from the apes strange.

He walked back to the front porch and sat down. His mind still saw the two giant mounds of red-orange fur moving together like one being.

When the two orangs came back around, Douglas thought he saw smugness in Vernon's face. Why not, he thought? I guess I would be smug, too.

Annie flopped down on the grassy front yard and crossed one leg over the other, her abdomen bulging high; she gazed upward into the heavy white sky.

Vernon bounded toward Douglas. He was young and red-chocolate-colored. His face was still slim, without the older orangutan jowls yet.

'Be polite,' Douglas warned him.

'Drink tea, please?' Vernon signed rapidly, the fringe on his elbows waving. 'Dry as bone.'

Douglas handed Vernon one of the glasses of tea, though he'd brought it out for Annie. The handsome 9-year-old downed it in a gulp. 'Thank you,' he signed. He touched the edge of the porch and withdrew his long fingers. 'Could fry egg,' he signed, and instead of sitting, swung out hand-over-hand on the ropes between the roof of the schoolhouse and the trees. It was a sparse and dry substitute for the orang's native rain forest.

He's too young and crude for Annie, Douglas thought.

'Annie,' Douglas called. 'Your tea.'

Annie rolled onto one side and lay propped on an elbow, staring at him. She was lovely. Fifteen years old, her fur was glossy and coppery, her small yellow eyes in the fleshy face expressive and intelligent. She started to rise up toward him, but turned toward the road.

The mail jeep was coming down the highway.

In a blurred movement, she set off at a four-point gallop down the half-mile drive toward the mailbox. Vernon swung down from his tree and followed, giving a small groan.

Reluctant to go out in the sun, Douglas put down the tea anyway and followed the apes along the drive. By the time he got near them, Annie was sitting with mail sorted between her toes, holding an opened letter in her hands. She looked up with an expression on her face that he'd never seen – it could have been fear, but it wasn't.

She handed the letter to Vernon, who pestered her for it. 'Douglas,' she signed, 'they want to buy my story.'

Therese lay in the bathwater, her knees sticking up high, her hair floating beside her face. Douglas sat on the edge of the tub; as he talked to her he was conscious that he spoke a double language – the one with his lips and the other with his hands.

'As soon as I called Ms Young, the magazine editor, and told her who Annie was, she got really excited. She asked me why we hadn't sent a letter explaining it with the story, so I told her that Annie didn't want anyone to know first.'

'Did Annie decide that?' Therese sounded skeptical, as she always seemed to when Douglas talked about Annie.

'We talked about it and she wanted it that way.' Douglas felt the resistance from Therese. Why she never understood, he didn't know, unless she did it to provoke him.

She acted as though she thought an ape was still just an ape, no matter what he or she could do. 'Anyway,' he said, 'she talked about doing a whole publicity thing to the hilt – talk shows, autograph parties. You know. But Dr Morris thinks it would be better to keep things quiet.'

'Why?' Therese sat up; her legs went underwater and she soaped her arms.

'Because she'd be too nervous. Annie, I mean. It might disrupt her education to become a celebrity. Too bad. Even Dr Morris knows that it would be great for fund-raising. But I guess we'll let the press in some.'

Therese began to shampoo her hair. 'I brought home that essay that Sandy wrote yesterday. The one I told you about. Now if she were an orangutan instead of just a deaf kid, she could probably get it published in *Fortune*.' Therese smiled.

Douglas stood. He didn't like the way Therese headed for the old argument – no matter what one of Therese's deaf students did, if Annie could do it one one-hundredth as well, it was more spectacular. Douglas knew it was true, but why Therese was so bitter about it, he didn't understand.

'That's great,' he said, trying to sound enthusiastic.

'Will you wash my back?' she asked.

He crouched and absent-mindedly washed her. 'I'll never forget Annie's face when she read that letter.'

'Thank you,' Therese said. She rinsed. 'Do you have any plans for this evening?'

'I've got work to do,' he said, leaving the bathroom. 'Would you like me to work in the bedroom so you can watch television?'

After a long pause, she said 'No, I'll read.'

He hesitated in the doorway. 'Why don't you go to sleep early? You look tired.'

She shrugged. 'Maybe I am.'

In the playroom at the school, Douglas watched Annie

closely. It was still morning, though late. In the recliner across the room from him, she seemed a little sleepy. Staring out the window, blinking, she marked her place in Pinkwater's *Fat Men From Space* with a long brown finger.

He had been thinking about Therese, who'd been silent and morose that morning. Annie was never morose, though often quiet. He wondered if Annie was quiet today because she sensed that Douglas was not happy. When he'd come to work, she'd given him an extra hug.

He wondered if Annie could have a crush on him, like many schoolgirls have on their teachers. Remembering her mating with Vernon days before, he idly wandered into a fantasy of touching those petals of her genitals and gently, gently moving inside her.

The physical reaction to his fantasy embarrassed him. *God, what am I thinking?* He shook himself out of the reverie, averting his gaze for a few moments, until he'd gotten control of himself again.

'Douglas,' Annie signed. She walked erect, towering, to him and sat down on the floor at his feet. Her flesh folded into her lap like dough.

'What?' he asked, wondering suddenly if orangutans were telepathic.

'Why you say my story children's?'

He looked blankly at her.

'Why not send *Harper's*?' she asked, having to spell out the name of the magazine.

He repressed a laugh, knowing it would upset her. 'It's . . . it's the kind of story children would like.'

'Why?'

He sighed. 'The level or writing is . . . *young*. Like you, sweetie.' He stroked her head, looking into the small, intense eyes. 'You'll get more sophisticated as you grow.'

'I smart as you,' she signed. 'You understand me always because I talk smart. You not always talk smart.'

Douglas was dumbfounded by her logic.

She tilted her head and waited. When Douglas shrugged,

she seemed to assume victory and returned to her recliner.

Dr Morris came in. 'Here we go,' she said, handing him the paper and leaving again.

Douglas skimmed the page until he came to an article about the 'ape author.' He scanned it. It contained one of her flashpoints; this and the fact that she was irritable from being in estrus made him consider hiding it. But that wouldn't be right.

'Annie,' he said softly.

She looked up.

'There's an article about you.'

'Me read,' she signed, putting her book on the floor. She came and crawled up on the sofa next to him. He watched her eyes as they jerked across every word. He grew edgy. She read on.

Suddenly she took off as if from a diving board. He ran after her as she bolted out the door. The stuffed dog which had always been a favorite toy was being shredded in those powerful hands even before he knew she had it. Annie screamed as she pulled the toy apart, running into the yard.

Terrified by her own aggression, she ran up the tree with stuffing falling like snow behind her.

Douglas watched as the shade filled with foam rubber and fake fur. The tree branches trembled. After a long while, she stopped pummeling the tree and sat quietly.

She spoke to herself with her long ape hand. 'Not animal,' she said, 'not animal.'

Douglas suddenly realized that Therese was afraid of the apes.

She watched warily as the four of them strolled along the edge of the school acreage. Douglas knew that Therese didn't appreciate the grace of Annie's muscular gait as he did; the sign language that passed between them was as similar to the Ameslan that Therese used for her deaf children as British to Jamaican. Therese couldn't appreciate Annie in creative conversation.

It wasn't good to be afraid of the apes, no matter how educated they were.

He had invited her out, hoping it would please her to be included in his world here. She had only visited briefly twice before.

Vernon lagged behind them, snapping pictures now and then with his expensive but hardy camera modified for his hands. Vernon took several pictures of Annie and one of Douglas, but only when Therese had separated from him to peer in between the rushes at the edge of the creek.

'Annie,' Douglas called, pointing ahead. 'A cardinal. The red bird.'

Annie lumbered forward. She glanced back to see where Douglas pointed, then stood still, squatting. Douglas walked beside her and they watched the bird.

It flew.

'Gone,' Annie signed.

'Wasn't it pretty, though?' Douglas asked.

They ambled on. Annie stopped often to investigate shiny bits of trash or large bugs. They rarely came this far from the school. Vernon whizzed past them, a dark auburn streak of youthful energy.

Remembering Therese, Douglas turned. She sat on a stump far behind. He was annoyed. He'd told her to wear her jeans and a straw hat because there would be grass burrs and hot sun. But there she sat, bare-headed, wearing shorts, miserably rubbing at her ankles.

He grunted impatiently. Annie looked up at him. 'Not you,' he said, stroking her fur. She patted his butt.

'Go on,' Douglas said, turning his back. When he came to Therese, he said, 'What's the problem?'

'No problem.' She started forward without looking at him. 'I was just resting.'

Annie had paused to poke at something on the ground with a stick. Douglas quickened his step. Even though his students were smart, they had orangutan appetites. He always worried that they would eat something that would sicken them. 'What is it?' he called.

'Dead cat,' Vernon signed back. He took a picture as Annie flipped the carcass with her stick.

Therese hurried forward. 'Oh, poor kitty,' she said, kneeling.

Annie had seemed too absorbed in poking the cat to notice Therese approach. Only a quick eye could follow her leap. Douglas was stunned.

Both screamed. It was over.

Annie clung to Douglas's legs, whimpering.

'Shit!' Therese said. She lay on the ground, rolling from side to side, holding her left arm. Blood dripped from between her fingers.

Douglas pushed Annie back. 'That was bad, *very bad*,' he said. 'Do you hear me?'

Annie sank down on her rump and covered her head. She hadn't gotten a child-scolding for a long time. Vernon stood beside her, shaking his head, signing, 'Not wise, baboon-face.'

'Stand up,' Douglas said to Therese. 'I can't help you right now.'

Therese was pale, but dry-eyed. Clumsily, she stood and grew even paler. A hunk of flesh hung loosely from above her elbow, meaty and bleeding. 'Look.'

'Go on. Walk back to the house. We'll come right behind you.' He tried to keep his voice calm, holding a warning hand on Annie's shoulder.

Therese moaned, catching her breath. 'It hurts,' she said, but stumbled on.

'We're coming,' Douglas said sternly. 'Just walk and – Annie, don't you dare step out of line.'

They walked silently, Therese ahead, leaving drops of blood in the dirt. The drops got larger and closer together. Once, Annie dipped her finger into a bloody spot and sniffed her fingertip.

Why can't things just be easy and peaceful, he wondered?

Something always happens. *Always.* He should have known better than to bring Therese around Annie. Apes didn't understand that vulnerable quality that Therese was made of. He himself didn't understand it, though at one time he'd probably been attracted to it. No – maybe he had never really seen it until it was too late. He'd only thought of Therese as 'sweet' until their lives were too tangled up to keep clear of it.

Why couldn't she be as tough as Annie? Why did she always take everything so seriously?

They reached the building. Douglas sent Annie and Vernon to their rooms and guided Therese to the infirmary. He watched as Jim, their all-purpose nurse and veterinary assistant examined her arm. 'I think you should probably have stitches.'

He left the room to make arrangements.

Therese looked at Douglas, holding the gauze over her still-bleeding arm. 'Why did she bite me?' she asked.

Douglas didn't answer. He couldn't think of how to express it.

'Do you have any idea?' she asked.

'You asked for it, all your wimping around.'

'I . . .'

Douglas saw the anger rising in her. He didn't want to argue now. He wished he'd never brought her. He'd done it all for her, and she had ruined it.

'Don't start,' he said simply, giving her a warning look.

'But, Douglas, I didn't do anything.'

'Don't start,' he repeated.

'I see now,' she said coldly. 'Somehow it's my fault again.'

Jim returned with his supplies.

'Do you want me to stay?' Douglas asked. He suddenly felt a pang of guilt, realizing that she was actually hurt enough for all this attention.

'No,' she said softly.

And her eyes looked far, far from him as he left her.

On the same day that the largest donation ever came to the school, a television news team came out to tape.

Douglas could tell that everyone was excited. Even the chimps that lived on the north half of the school hung on the fence and watched the TV van being unloaded. The reporter decided upon the playroom as the best location for the taping, though she didn't seem to relish sitting on the floor with the giant apes. People went over scripts, strung cords and microphones, set up hot lights, and discussed angles and sound while pointing at the high ceiling's jungle-gym design. All this to talk to a few people and an orangutan.

They brought Annie's desk into the playroom, contrary to Annie's wishes. Douglas explained that it was temporary, that these people would go away after they talked a little. Douglas and Annie stayed outside as long as possible and played Tarzan around the big tree. He tickled her. She grabbed him as he swung from a limb. 'Kagoda?' she signed, squeezing him with one arm.

'Kagoda!' he shouted, laughing.

They relaxed on the grass. Douglas was hot. He felt flushed all over. 'Douglas,' Annie signed, 'they read story?'

'Not yet. It isn't published yet.'

'Why talk me?'

'Because you wrote it and sold it and people like to interview famous authors.' He groomed her shoulder. 'Time to go in,' he said, seeing a wave from inside.

Annie picked him up in a big hug and carried him in.

'Here it is!' Douglas called to Therese, and turned on the video-recorder.

First, a long shot of the school from the dusty drive, looking only functional and square, without personality. The reporter's voice said, 'Here, just south-east of town, is a special school with unusual young students. The students here have little prospect for employment when they graduate, but millions of dollars each year fund this institution.'

A shot of Annie at her typewriter, picking at the keyboard with her long fingers; a sheet of paper is slowly covered with large block letters.

'This is Annie, a 15-year-old orangutan, who has been a student with the school for five years. She graduated with honors from another 'ape school' in Georgia before coming here. And now Annie has become a writer. Recently, she sold a story to a children's magazine. The editor who bought the story didn't know that Annie was an orangutan until after she had selected the story for publication.'

Annie looked at the camera uncertainly.

'Annie can read and write and understand spoken English, but she cannot speak. She uses a sign language similar to the one hearing-impaired use.' Change in tone from narrative to interrogative. 'Annie, how did you start writing?'

Douglas watched himself on the small screen watching Annie sign, 'Teacher told me write.' He saw himself grin, eyes shift slightly toward the camera, but generally watching Annie. His name and 'Orangutan Teacher' appeared on the screen. The scene made him uneasy.

'What made you send in Annie's story for publication?' the reporter asked.

Douglas signed to Annie, she came to him for a hug, and turned a winsome face to the camera. 'Our administrator, Dr Morris, and I both thought it was as good as any kids' story, so Dr Morris said, "Send it in." The editor liked it.' Annie nervously made 'pee' sign to Douglas.

Then, a shot of Dr Morris in her office, a chimp on her lap, clapping her brown hands.

'Dr Morris, your school was established five years ago by grants and government funding. What is your purpose here?'

'Well, in the last few decades, apes – mostly chimpanzees like Rose here – have been taught sign language experimentally. Mainly to prove that apes could indeed use

language.' Rosie put the tip of her finger through the gold
hoop in Dr Morris's ear. Dr Morris took her hand away
gently. 'We were established with the idea of *educating* apes,
a comparable education to the primary grades.' She looked
at the chimp. 'Or however far they will advance.'

'Your school has two orangutans and six chimpanzees.
Are there differences in their learning?' the reporter asked.

Dr Morris nodded emphatically. 'Chimpanzees are very
clever, but the orang has a different brain structure which
allows for more abstract reasoning. Chimps learn many
things quickly, orangs are slower. But the orangutan has
the ability to learn in greater depth.'

Shot of Vernon swinging on the ropes in front of the
school.

Assuming that Vernon is Annie, the reporter said, 'Her
teacher felt from the start that Annie was an especially
promising student. The basic sentences that she types
out on her typewriter are simple but original entertainment.'

Another shot of Annie at the typewriter.

'If you think this is just monkey business, you'd better
think again. Tolstoy, watch out!'

Depressed by the lightness, brevity, and the stupid
'monkey business' remark, Douglas turned off the television.

He sat for a long time. Whenever Therese had gone to
bed, she had left him silently. After half an hour of staring
at the blank screen, he rewound his video-recorder and ran
it soundlessly until Annie's face appeared.

And then froze it. He could almost feel again the softness
of her halo of red hair against his chin.

He couldn't sleep.

Therese had rumpled her way out of the sheet and lay on
her side, her back to him. He looked at the shape of her
shoulder and back, downward to the dip of the waist, up
the curve of her hip. Her buttocks were round ovals, one

atop the other. Her skin was sleek and shiny in the filtered street light coming through the window. She smelled slightly of shampoo and even more slightly of female.

What he felt for her, when he thought of her generally, anyone could call love. And yet, he found himself helplessly angry with her most of the time. When he thought he could amuse her, it would end with her feelings being hurt for some obscure reason. He heard cruel words come barging out of an otherwise gentle mouth. She took everything seriously; mishaps and misunderstandings occurred beyond his control, beyond his repair.

Under this satiny skin, she was troubled and tense. A lot of sensitivity and fear. He had stopped trying to gain access to what had been the happier parts of her person, not understanding where they had gone. He had stopped wanting to love her, but he didn't *not* want to love her, either. It just did not seem to matter.

Sometimes, he thought, it would be easier to have someone like Annie for a wife.

Annie.

He loved her furry face. He loved the unconditional joy in her face when she saw him. She was bright and warm and unafraid. She didn't read things into what he said, but listened and talked with him. They were so natural together. Annie was so filled with vitality.

Douglas withdrew his hand from Therese, whose skin seemed a bare blister of dissatisfaction.

He lay on the floor of the apes' playroom with the fan blowing across his chest. He held Annie's report on Lawrence's *Sons and Lovers* by diagonal corners to keep it from flapping.

Annie lazily swung from bars criss-crossing the ceiling.

'Paul wasn't happy at work because the boss looked over his shoulder at his handwriting,' she had written. 'But he was happy again later. His brother died and his mother was sad. Paul got sick. He was better and visited his friends again. His mother died and his friends didn't tickle him any more.'

Douglas looked over the top of the paper at Annie. True, it was the first time she'd read an 'adult' novel, but he had expected something better than this. He considered asking her if Vernon had written the report for her, but thought better of it.

'Annie,' he said, sitting up. 'What do you think this book is really about?'

She swung down and landed on the sofa. 'About man,' she said.

Douglas waited. There was no more. 'But what about it? Why this man instead of another? What was special about him?'

Annie rubbed her hands together, answerless.

'What about his mother?'

'She help him,' Annie answered in a flurry of dark fingers. 'Especially when he paint.'

Douglas frowned. He looked at the page again, disappointed.

'What I do?' Annie asked, worried.

He tried to brighten up. 'You did just fine. It was a hard book.'

'Annie smart,' the orang signed. 'Annie smart.'

Douglas nodded. 'I know.'

Annie rose, then stood on her legs, looking like a two-story fuzzy building, teetering from side to side. 'Annie smart. Writer. Smart,' she signed. 'Write book. Bestseller.'

Douglas made a mistake. He laughed. Not as simple as a human laughing at another, this was an act of aggression. His bared teeth and uncontrolled guff-guff struck out at Annie. He tried to stop.

She made a gulping sound and galloped out of the room.

'Wait, Annie!' He chased after her.

By the time he got outside she was far ahead. He stopped running when his chest hurt and trotted slowly through the weeds toward her. She sat forlornly far away and watched him come.

When he was near, she signed 'hug' three times.

Douglas collapsed, panting, his throat raw. 'Annie, I'm sorry,' he said. 'I didn't mean it.' He put his arms around her.

She held onto him.

'I love you, Annie. I love you so much I don't want ever to hurt you. Ever, ever, ever. I want to be with you all the time. Yes, you're smart and talented and good.' He kissed her tough face.

Whether forgotten or forgiven, the hurt of his laughter was gone from her eyes. She held him tighter, making a soft sound in her throat, a sound for him.

They lay together in the crackling yellow weeds, clinging. Douglas felt his love physically growing for her. More passionately than ever before in his life, he wanted to make love to her. He touched her. He felt that she understood what he wanted, that her breath on his neck was anticipation. A consummation as he'd never imagined, the joining of their species in language and body. Not dumb animal-banging but mutual love . . . He climbed over her and hugged her back.

Annie went rigid when he entered her.

Slowly, she rolled away from him, but he held onto her. 'No.' A horrible grimace came across her face that raised the hairs on the back of Douglas's neck. 'Not you,' she said.

She's going to kill me, he thought.

His passion declined; Annie disentangled herself and walked away.

He sat for a moment, stunned at what he'd done, at what had happened, wondering what he would do for the rest of his life with the memory of it. Then he zipped up his pants.

Staring at his dinner plate, he thought, it's just the same as if I had been rejected by a woman.

His hands could still remember the matted feel of her fur; tucked in his groin was the memory of being in an alien place. It had made him throw up out in the field that afternoon, and afterwards he'd come straight home. He hadn't even said good night to the orangs.

'What's the matter?' Therese asked.

He shrugged.

She half-rose out of her chair to kiss him on the temple. 'You don't have a fever, do you?'

'No.'

'Can I do something to make you feel better?' Her hand slid along his thigh.

He stood up. 'Stop it.'

She sat still. 'Are you in love with another woman?'

Why can't she just leave me alone. 'No. I have a lot on my mind.'

'It never was like this, even when you were working on your thesis.'

'Therese,' he said, with what he felt was undeserved patience, 'just leave me alone. It doesn't help with you at me all the time.'

'But I'm scared. I don't know what to do. You act like you don't want me around.'

'All you do is criticize me.' He stood and took his dishes to the sink.

Slowly, she trailed after him, carrying her plate. 'I'm just trying to understand. It's my life, too.'

He said nothing and she walked away as if someone had told her not to leave footsteps.

In the bathroom, he stripped and stood under the shower for a long time. He imagined that Annie's smell clung to him. He felt that Therese could smell it on him.

What have I done, what have I done . . . ?

And when he came out of the shower, Therese was gone.

He had considered calling in sick, but he knew that it would be just as miserable to stay around the house and think about Annie, think about Therese, and worse, to think about himself.

He dressed for work, but couldn't eat breakfast. Realizing that his pain showed, he straightened his shoulders, but found them drooping again as he got out of the car at work.

With some fear, he came through the office. The secretary greeted him with rolling eyes. 'Someone's given out our number again,' she said as the phone buzzed. Another line was on hold. 'This morning there was a man standing at the window watching me until Gramps kicked him off the property.'

Douglas shook his head in sympathy with her and approached the orang's door. He felt nauseated again.

Vernon sat at his typewriter, composing captions for his photo album. He didn't get up to greet Douglas, but gave him an evaluative stare.

Douglas patted his shoulder. 'Working?' he asked.

'Like dog,' Vernon said and returned to typing.

Annie sat outside on the back porch. Douglas opened the door and stood beside her. She looked up at him, but – like Vernon – made no move toward the customary hug. The morning was still cool, the shadow of the building still long in front of them. Douglas sat down.

'Annie,' he said softly. 'I'm sorry. I'll never do it again. You see, I felt . . .' He stopped. It wasn't any easier than it had been to talk to Oona, or Wendy, or Shelley, or Therese . . . He realized then that he didn't understand her any more than he'd understood them. Why had she rejected him? What was she thinking? What would happen from now on? Would they be friends again?

'Oh, hell,' he said. He stood. 'It won't happen again.'

Annie gazed away into the trees.

He felt strained all over, especially in his throat. He stood by her a long time.

'I don't want write stories,' she signed.

Douglas stared at her. 'Why?'

'Don't want.' She seemed to shrug.

Douglas wondered what had happened to the confident ape who'd planned to write a bestseller the day before. 'Is that because of me?'

She didn't answer.

'I don't understand,' he said. 'Do you want to write it down for me? Could you explain it that way?'

'No,' she signed, 'can't explain. Don't want.'

He continued. 'What *do* you want?'

'Sit tree. Eat bananas, chocolate. Drink brandy.' She looked at him seriously. 'Sit tree. Day, day, day, week, month, year.'

Christ almighty, he thought, she's having a goddamned existential crisis. All the years of education. All the accomplishments. The hopes of an entire field of primatology. All shot to hell because of a moody ape. It can't just be me. This would have happened sooner or later, maybe . . . He thought of all the effort he would have to make to repair their relationship. It made him tired.

'Annie, why don't we just ease up a little on your work. You can rest today. You can go sit in the trees all of today and I'll bring you a glass of wine.'

She shrugged again.

Oh, I've botched it, he thought. What an idiot. He felt a pain coming back, a pain like poison, with a focal point but shooting through his heart and hands, making him dizzy and short of breath.

At least she doesn't hate me, he thought, squatting to touch her hand.

She bared her teeth.

Douglas froze. She slid away from him and headed for the trees.

He sat alone at home and watched the newscast. In a small midwestern town they burned the issues of the magazine with Annie's story in it.

A heavy woman in a windbreaker was interviewed with the bonfire in the background. 'I don't want my children reading things that weren't even written by humans. I have human children and this godless ape is not going to tell its stories to them.'

A quick interview with Dr Morris, who looked even more tired and introverted than usual. 'The story is a very innocent tale, told by an innocent personality. I really don't think she has any ability or intention to corrupt . . .'

He turned the television off. He picked up the phone and dialed one of Therese's friends. 'Jan, have you heard from Therese yet?'

'No, sure haven't.'

'Well, let me know, okay?'

'Sure.'

He thought vaguely about trying to catch her at work, but he left earlier in the morning and came home later in the evening than she did.

Looking at her pictures on the wall, he thought of when they had first met, first lived together. There had been a time when he had loved her so much, he'd been bursting with it. Now he felt empty. He didn't want her to hate him, but he still didn't know if he could talk to her about what had happened. The idea that she would sit and listen to him didn't seem realistic.

Even Annie wouldn't listen to him any more.

He was alone. He'd done a big, dumb, terrible thing. It would have been different if Annie had reciprocated, if somehow they could have become lovers. Then it would have been them against the world, a new kind of relationship.

But Annie didn't seem any different to Therese when it really came down to it. She didn't have any more interest in him than Dr Morris would have in Vernon. He'd imagined it.

He was alone. And without Annie's consent, he was just a jerk who'd fucked an ape.

'I made a mistake,' he said aloud to Therese's picture. 'So let's forget it.'

But he couldn't forget.

'Dr Morris wants to see you,' the secretary said as he came in.

'Okay.' He changed course for the administrative office. He whistled. In the past few days, Annie had been cool, but he felt that everything would settle down eventually. He felt better. Wondering what horrors or marvels Dr Morris had to share with him, he knocked at her door and peered through the glass window. Probably another magazine burning, he thought.

She signaled him to come in. 'Hello, Douglas.'

Annie, he thought, *something's happened.*

He stood until she motioned him to sit down. She looked at his face for several seconds. 'This is difficult for me,' she said.

She's found out, he thought. But he put that aside, figuring it was a paranoia that made him worry. There's no way. No way. I have to calm down or I'll show it.

She held up a photograph.

There it was – a dispassionate and cold document of that one moment in his life. She held it up to him like an accusation. It shocked him as if it hadn't been himself.

Defiance forced him to stare at the picture instead of looking for compassion in Dr Morris's eyes. He knew exactly where the picture had come from.

Vernon and his new telephoto lens.

He visualized the image of his act rising up in a tray of chemicals. Slowly, he looked away from it. Dr Morris could not know how he had changed since that moment. He could make no protest or denial.

'I have no choice,' Dr Morris said flatly. 'I'd always thought that even if you weren't good with people, at least you worked well with the apes. Thank God Henry, who does Vernon's darkroom work, has promised not to say anything.'

Douglas was rising from his chair. He wanted to tear the

picture out of her hands. He didn't want her to see it. He wanted her to ask him if he had changed, let him reassure her that it would never happen again, that he understood he'd been wrong.

But her eyes were flat and shuttered against him. 'We'll send your things,' she said.

He paused at his car and saw two big red shapes – one coppery orange, one chocolate-red – sitting in the trees. Vernon bellowed out a groan that ended with an alien burbling. It was a wild sound full of the jungle and steaming rain.

Douglas watched Annie scratch herself and look toward some chimps walking the land beyond their boundary fence. As she started to turn her gaze in his direction, he ducked into his car.

I guess an ape wouldn't understand me any more than a human, he thought, angrily trying to drive his shame away.